J.A. Tuero retired at the end of 2018. He was a professional in the field of mechanical design and engineering, for 37 out of 43 years. Some of the job positions included, electro-mechanical designer working at a research and development facility contributing to high-definition television, non-destructive ultra-sound testing, spatial-temporal participation for NASA space dementia studies used prior to the construction of the international space station, mechanical designer for safety and rescue equipment, technical drafting designer for aerospace defense companies. On January 2017, J.A. Tuero received his United States Patent for the Thrust Enabling Objective System (T.E.O.S.). Now he dedicates his effort to writing short stories, fiction, romantic, and comedy novels. The latest fiction thriller he penned is about preventing a mega-tsunami, should the Cumbre Vieja mountain top on Las Palmas, Canary Islands slides into the ocean.

I lost my younger sister, Michelle, to cancer in May of 2016. On the day she passed away, she took a piece of my heart with her. I always enjoyed her impromptu visits on Saturday nights. Fresh coffee was ready to be served as soon as she arrived. We would spend hours discussing every subject from astronomy to zoology. She was my greatest advocate that championed the invention. I miss you, little sister! Look down on me and be proud. I love you always.

J.A. Tuero

THE TAKE-DOWN INITIATIVE

TRIUMPH AND TRAGEDY

AUSTIN MACAULEY PUBLISHERS™

LONDON • CAMBRIDGE • NEW YORK • SHARJAH

Ordering Information
Quantity sales: Special discounts are available on quantity purchases by corporations, associations, and others. For details, contact the publisher at the address below.

Publisher's Cataloging-in-Publication data
Tuero, J.A.
The Take-Down Initiative

ISBN 9781643787961 (Paperback)
ISBN 9781643787978 (Hardback)
ISBN 9781643787985 (ePub e-book)

Library of Congress Control Number: 2021900916

www.austinmacauley.com/us

First Published (2021)
Austin Macauley Publishers LLC
40 Wall Street, 33rd Floor, Suite 3302
New York, NY 10005
USA

mail-usa@austinmacauley.com
+1 (646) 5125767

It's important that I give recognition to those who inspired me, awakening the dormant skills that I possessed. It's only fair that my teachers and mentors revel in the satisfaction that their contributions made a difference to the quality of the end product. My dearest and sincerest thanks to all my English literary teachers both in high school and in college. Without their guidance and firm commitments to the doctrines of better teaching, this book would not have been possible. Thank you to all who taught me well.

Introduction

I'm a firm advocate of what is made to serve good, can equally be made to serve bad. This book is about an incredible invention designed to support an alternative for commercial airliners, private and military aircrafts alike. Meant to protect and save lives, thus keeping terrible unforeseen air tragedies at bay.

What happens when you think that all is right in the world; then you're suddenly faced with the terrible dilemma that you're between a threshold, in a balance between life and death? No longer do you have a voice in deciding your outcome. The decision is moot due to the overwhelming fact that there are external forces in control.

On a terrible and tragic eleventh day of September 2001, all those souls onboard four airliners, two world trade center buildings in NYC, and the Pentagon in Washington D.C. never anticipated to be assassinated merely on personal religious beliefs compelling a group of zealots to commit murder in the name of God.

Just to avenge a false idiosyncrasy whose only consequence would forever bring total discordance to families that lost loved ones brutally murdered on that day.

Now, what if a more powerful faction we respect to be the highest authority in the land can wheel a similar sword of righteous damnation where tormentors and tormented alike would suffer the same fate. In the end, the method to the demise will be the same for all.

As I draw closer towards the end of this introduction. I would like to summit a question for all the readers. This may be interpreted as a simple "yes" or "no" question.

As we have seen and been witness to in the past, anytime an airliner is taken over by force, everyone immediately labels the perpetrators as hijackers or terrorists.

Then all those that have their rights and freedoms violated are called the victims. Now comes my question:

In order to stop the terrorists, do we simply turn a blind eye having the airliner shot down by a military jet fighter?

If anyone of us would agree to having the airliner shot down, we would be no better than the terrorists. They focus on a target then fly into it. The terrorists die with the good graces of Allah, while the innocent victims die in vain.

What if a system existed that can do two things? Keep the terrorists from accomplishing their objective yet still save the plane with all its innocent passengers onboard?

Read this book, you will see that at some point, it's possible to foil the terrorists, save the plane and the passengers.

Enjoy and good reading. Thank you.

Chapter 1

Three o'clock in the morning. Quiet enough to hear a pin drop and a fly scurry across the floor looking for an abandoned cake crumb. Tracy Sherman, Joe's wife, was in peaceful repose when she suddenly woke. There was someone missing in the bed; it was her husband Joe. She reaches over to the night table, turning on the light. Darting a glance back over to the right side of the bed, she quickly notices that Joe was not in bed. She surmised that he must have felt asleep again at the computer.

Tracy Sherman, 47, five foot and two inches tall, slender face and body, beautiful long flowing blonde hair, with the most exquisite pair of eyes you could ever peer at. One look from those eyes could hypnotize any man at will. There would be no doubt that her gaze could reach deep into a man's soul stirring emotions that were not felt before.

Tracy was the adherence that Joe could always depend on. She would never waiver; hold steadfast by him through good and bad. He was so proud and grateful of his beautiful adoring wife.

Tracy silently gets up from her side of the bed. She knew that if he didn't get a good night's rest, he would be nothing more than a lethargic zombie for the better part of the day.

She tiptoes into Joe's study, slowing, cautiously approaching him from his right, making sure not to bump into his desk. Doing that would surely startle him, scaring him out of his skin. Tracy came over to where Joe had laid his head down on the mouse pad and was out like a light. His computer still had three dimensional files open, still working on one section of his invention. Tracy carefully, precariously leaning over to Joe's right ear, keeping about an inch or two from his head as she whispered ever so faintly, "Joe, Joe honey get up and go to bed." It took a moment for Joe's synapses to reconnect after such a peaceful somnolent sojourn. Joe slowly raised his head, turned his head to the right, looked over at Tracy with the most god awful quirkily look on his face.

Joe smacks his mouth, sloshing his tongue around the inside as he tries to muster up some much-needed saliva. It was obvious that he slept the whole time with his mouth open. "How long have I been asleep?" as he looks at Tracy with droopy sleep filled eyes.

"I'm not sure, honey. Do you remember when you came into the study to work on your invention?"

Joe, "I think about twelve thirty,"

Tracy, "It's pass three in the morning. If you don't come to bed now, you're going to feel it, it will hit you like a ton of bricks." Tracy affirmed with a degree of sternness in her voice.

"Okay," Joe said, "I'm coming to bed." Tracy reached over taking Joe's right arm as she helped him to get up from his executive chair. She walked Joe out of the study, flipping off the light switch as they crossed the threshold out into the hallway. Tracy skillfully maneuvered Joe down the hall, making a right turn into their bedroom. She walked Joe to his side of the bed, sat him down on the edge, as she started to take his clothes off. After Tracy removed his shoes and socks, she picks both of Joe's legs swinging them to the left until he was squarely on his side of the bed. She then grabbed his pants on either side, slowly shimmied his pants down his legs until they came off as she placed them on the storage chest in front of their bed along with his shirt.

"Okay, now get some sleep," Tracy demanded. "Don't forget to take a shower before you go to work in the morning, stinky! Luckily, I'm changing the sheets in the morning so you can sleep on the used ones for tonight."

Joe turned his head to the right, looking up at those beautiful blue eyes that sparkled in the faint light of the bedroom, saying, "Yes, dear, I'll get some sleep." Adding, "Thank you, honey, what would I do without you?"

"Well, you would probably do most of your sleeping in the study, with your head propped on a mouse pad." Tracy leaned over, giving Joe a kiss on the forehead, saying, "Goodnight, sleep well."

Joe had set his mind over the long holiday of Memorial Day weekend to complete his patent drawings. Submit them along with the written part of the patent application to the United States Patent and Trademark Office. As he was intensely concentrated, fiercely staring into the monitor screen, Tracy decided to pay Joe an impromptu visit to investigate how he was progressing. She quietly walked up to the back of the monitor, crouching down like a cat on the prowl, where her head was covered by the top of the

13

monitor. She slowly lifted her head exposing her face while Joe was still staring so intensely. Tracy leaned forward over the monitor like a giraffe reaching for a tasting morsel of acacia leaves; just stared until Joe's peripheral caught sight of Tracy slender face as she revealed a big wide smile.

"Hi there, beautiful," Joe blurred out in a chirper voice.

"Hi back," Tracy exclaimed as she looked at Joe with her sparkling blue eyes. "How are you coming along?" Tracy asking inquisitively.

"There is still much to do, but I can't sit on my hands with this. It can sometimes take up to 36 months before I see a patent number from the USPTO if they grant it."

"I don't see why not, Joe," Tracy exclaimed in a positive and assertive voice. "You have worked so long on this project for it not to make it."

"I know I have, honey, a lot of times industry doesn't like when a rogue like me comes up with a new and revolutionary idea their engineers didn't think of first." The company response is to reject the idea completely.

"Oh, well," Tracy blasted out in a sarcastic manner. "So, no one other than large industry can claim the right to invent something to help keep mankind safe?"

Joe goes on to comment, "You see, honey, large companies, like aerospace, have a lot to gain and more to lose. They compete with other companies to stay on top of the technology game. If they don't come up with a great new idea or product that they can introduce to the world or to the government, then it's not worth their time and effort to explore or develop; it's about the Benjamin's, bottom line."

"That just sucks," Tracy yelled out with a pout on her face. "Oh, the hell with it, tell me again how you came up with the idea for the Thrust Enabling Objective System, did I say it right?"

"Yes, you did, my dear," Joe looking up at Tracy with a proud grin on his face. "Come around, get behind my chair, I'll tell you."

Tracy walked around to the back of Joe's executive chair, leaning over folding her arms around his chest.

"Remember that one year, for my birthday, we decided to take the family on a Saint Augustine weekend at the old part of the city?"

Tracy chimes in, "Yeah, I remember, we had a great time there."

Joe continued telling the story, "We had to stop one time while on the road to make a pit stop at the rest area. Josh and I went into the men's lavatory to take care of business. I went over to wash my hands, after I washed my hands, I put my hands under the hand jet dryer. As I looked down, at my hands I had an epiphany; I saw my invention come to life. I remember saying to myself, *Oh my God*."

Joe looked over at Josh, saying, "I have to tell you guys something I have just experienced. I'll tell you when we get back in the car."

Joe and the family got in the car, Josh excitedly asked, "Okay, Dad, what got you so excited, are you going to tell us?"

"Let me back up the car and I'll tell you when we're back on the highway." Joe re-enters the highway, turning the radio down, saying, "You ready?"

Tracy, Josh and younger daughter Laura said almost in unison, "Yes, Dad, we're ready to hear the news!"

"I just had what a lot of people would claim to be what's called an epiphany."

Daughter Laura, 16, long blonde wavy hair, cute as a button, smart as a whip, curiously asked, "What's an epiphany?"

Joe answers, "An epiphany is an occurrence or experience where sometimes you don't know where it came from, but it alters your life or way of thinking."

Tracy rings in and asks, "Has it changed your life or way of thinking, honey?"

Joe answers, "Philosophically, I believe it has. It is imperative that I go with it to invent what I saw in my mind's eye."

Josh, 17, sandy blonde hair, athletic build, very much admired by his fellow classmates in school, poses the question to his father, "Dad, have you ever invented anything before?"

Joe turns his head, his lips skewed to the left, ever so slightly, so not to lose sight of the road, barking out, "What'a you kidding, Josh? Do you know how many companies I have worked for where I had to come up with new product design ideas. Including reverse engineering of products developed by competitors. Listen, it's about time that I invented something for myself and was able to get the credit for it, since I never did by the companies I worked for. This one is *mine* and I'll be damned if I'm going to let a pack of rotating steely-toothed company "Langoliers", (*Steven King's, the Langoliers, 1990*) rip me to shreds, threatening any chances of my invention making a difference in the world of aeronautics. Go tell that to the dead of an airliner full of people about to fly into a thunderstorm with hail the size of baseballs, like Southern Airways flight 242 in 1977."

Back in Joe's study, Tracy arms still around his chest, remembers Joe making a statement while in the car on the way to Saint Augustine.

"If my invention could someday save a plane load of people from crashing into the ground, but yet I decide to abandon the idea, I would be so terrible and pathetic of a human being not to follow through all the way."

Tracy pompously boasting, "We will be very proud of you, Joe. However you pursue this, we will wholeheartedly support your goals."

Joe leaning slightly forward in his chair, brimming a big smile tells Tracy, "You guys have been my biggest supporters and have put up with a lot of times that I would lock myself in the study just to get as much as I could accomplished. I thank you all for that. I promise that I will somehow make it up to all of you. I have asked for so much, and have given back so little," Joe affirms. "Don't worry, honey. Someday I hope there's a calling for my invention, putting it to good use."

Tracy exclaims, "I'm sure some aerospace company will want to give your idea a chance to grow into something spectacular."

"Speaking of spectacular," Joe reminds himself, "I better get back to finishing up my drawings or jet engines may no longer exist by the time I get my patent number."

For the next couple of weekends, rest and relaxation was not on Joe's agenda. Spending a couple of quiet days every weekend before heading back into work Monday morning was not a self-serving luxury he could afford.

On one particular weekend while working on his invention, he noticed a fault in his design that would raise many questions at the USPTO plus make his idea non-functional. He saw the deficiency, immediately correcting his drawings to reflect the change, then going through page after page of his patent application, changing both text with item callout numbers to correctly identify the improved parts in the assemblies. Joe finally has everything he needs wrapped up and ready to be submitted. Early on Wednesday morning before starting work, he logs in to the USPTO to submit his patent application online. Afterwards, he would have to wait to see what more the USPTO would require and what else they'd find wrong. Joe knows, it's a long trek whether the outcome of his invention will be accepted and granted for a patent number. It's all in the hands of a greater power. But he truly is a happy man by doing all he has had to do to put in his invention.

Monday morning, back at work. Joe walks into the cafeteria to grab a cup of coffee while on mid-morning break. He maneuvers around the cafeteria until he spots a small table unoccupied at one end of the room. He sits there in deep thought with his cup of coffee wrapped around his hands. The cafeteria was bustling with people walking in and out, talking, laughing, coffee pots clinging and clanging, making it hard to gather one's thoughts should there be the need.

While Joe was still in thought, his good friend and fellow co-worker Morgan Shepherd—48, tall, sandy blonde hair, with a deep tan and a smile that every woman in the company commented about at one time or another—approaches the table, putting his hand on Joe's back saying, "Hey, good morning, buddy."

Joe breaks his glare looking up at Morgan saying, "Hi there, how are you?"

Morgan replies, "As well as to be expected for a Monday morning."

"I hear that, have a seat," says Joe breaking into a friendly grin.

"So, what's going on with you Joe?"

"Well, I can't believe that it is coming up on two years since I got the patent number for T.E.O.S. Have you gotten any feedback from anyone for your invention?" Morgan asks inquisitively.

"I know there's got to be companies out there somewhere that would be willing to take a chance on my invention," Joe replies with a positive posture. Joe adds, "Maybe I could do a formal presentation, generate a series of slides I can put on social media for everyone to see. That way more people will have a chance to study how my invention works."

Morgan excitedly comments, "If they like it, they can tell others about it."

"Exactly," Joe boasted. "I need just one break to give my idea a jump start to get it going. I got to get off my butt and make this happen."

Morgan gets up, excusing himself, saying, "I better get back before they dock my pay," grabbing the back of the chair and sliding it into the table, as he looks at Joe with a devilish smirk.

Joe counters with, "Yeah, me too, I need to get back to work."

As Morgan is leaving the cafeteria, he turns quickly adding, "Joe, let me know if a company reaches out about your invention."

"I will my friend", as Joe watches his friend exit the cafeteria.

Just as Joe stands, ready to slide his chair under the table, his supervisor Sam comes into the cafeteria, spotting Joe as he walks over. Sam Stamos, 56, a bit short and paunchy, sometimes with an odd unlikely demeanor approaches Joe asking if he would stay later tonight to finish up a design. "It must be ready to be electronically sent over to China before their workday begins in about three hours."

Joe, looking quite annoyed, tries to reason with Sam on whether they really needed these designs tonight.

"Look, Joe, this was not my idea. The boys in the marketing department want the new designs heading out the door before our competitors get theirs going."

"Okay, let me see what I can do," as Joe begrudgingly conceits to the situation he has been forced into.

"Thanks, Joe, that's great!" as Sam grabs Joe's right hand giving it a hardy shake. "I'll go tell the boys in marketing that you'll bang that out tonight and get it to China."

Joe thinks to himself for a moment realizing that refusing to finish a project and pushing it out the door would only hurt his chances of a promotion (maybe?) or a pay increase. He had to bite his lower lip not go with the punches. He was secure in the fact that no matter what, his invention was patented and could do anything he wanted with it. Joe starts what he didn't finish, by sliding his chair under the table as he headed back to his office. As he passes one of the conference rooms on the way back, the marketing department was having their daily organizationally rally meetings. As Joe passed by the door, the marketing manager holding the meeting, Nathan Silvers, 37, medium build, black hair, parted to the side called out Joe's name.

Joe stopped, as he looked back into the doorway as Nathan got up greeting Joe by the conference room door. "Hey Joe, thanks a lot. I know that what we're asking of you is in very short notice. We need those designs in China ASAP. The Telex Company is gaining on us and the company can't afford to have any further delays in starting a pre-production run."

"No problem," said Joe confidently. "The main part of the sub-assemblies with the top-level assemblies are just about complete. Just a matter of looking everything over, zipping all the files, sending them over to Thomas Chang in Shenzhen."

"Great, Joe. Couldn't get anyone better to get this completed then one of our senior-most members in the company. I better let you go or none of this will happen when it should."

Joe and Nathan shook hands as Joe headed back to his office. As he walked towards his office he recalled Nathan's praise of him saying, "who better to get this completed than one of our most senior members in the company." *I never did get a thank you, so I guess that was the best I can get.* Joe shook his head, with a Mona Lisa type smile as he turns the corner into his office.

Chapter 2

Joe walks through the garage on his way to reaching the door leading into the kitchen. He intently looks down as he snakes his way through stacked boxes filled with Christmas ornaments on the floor. He carefully scrutinizes the path, making sure that no loose skateboards or a rogue pair of sneakers await to ensnare him as he walks through the dimly lit garage.

After successfully trekking the mine field of obstacles in the garage he successfully transverses towards the door to the kitchen, turning the knob to step in. He swings the door open, spotting wife Tracy preparing dinner, saying, "Hi honey."

Tracy looks back over her right shoulder and replies, "Hi, sweetheart how was work today?"

"Ah! You know, same old same old. Another day, another dollar," Joe answers nonchalantly, walking over delivering a tender peck on Tracy's right cheek.

Tracy turns to alert Joe, "You got a letter from R&R Industries addressed to you, it's by the front door console."

"Thanks honey, I'll go check it out now."

He walks over to the console. Picks up the letter, carefully opening it as if he was checking for an exploding envelope full of anthrax powder. He composes his glare squarely to scan the letter, line by line as if he was trying to decipher a secret message inside.

Putting the letter down on top of the console, he looks up at the ceiling, clinches both of his fist, bringing both his arms slightly above his head, projecting out a loud victory yell, "*Yes!*" as he dances around in a tight circle, ecstatic after reading the great news.

"Joe, is there anything wrong? Tracy asks with concern in her voice."

"No, honey! All our dreams have just come true," Joe announces with jubilation. "One of the companies I submitted my patent submission to, R&R Industries, wants to develop my invention. They are ready to discuss the licensing terms." Joe walks into the kitchen sitting down at the table.

"That's wonderful, Joe, I'm so happy and proud of you. You finally did it," Tracy says in an exuberant voice.

Joe prepares Tracy for the downside of not being able to be with her and the family. "You realize that I'll probably be travelling a lot; will have to be at R&R Industries for weeks at a time while the project is being researched and developed. I promise that I will call you every night, no matter how tired I am when I get back to my hotel room, I'll call you to check in on you and the kids."

"Joe, it's okay if your too tired to talk to me," Tracy reaffirms understandably. "Your commitment towards this company is paramount. You can't just say, 'I'm leaving early for the day so I can call my wife and kids back at the hotel.' We'll be fine, we know where you are."

"Yeah, you're right, honey. I'm sure they want to get their money's worth out of me," Joe bellows out.

"Joe, did that letter explain what the next step will be in getting your invention going with R&R Industries?" Tracy curiously asking.

"Here, I'll tell you what. Let me go get the letter, it's still on the console and you can read it for yourself." Joe walks to the front foyer picking up the letter from R&R Industries that was still unfolded out after Joe read it.

"Go ahead, honey, read it out loud if you like, I don't mind having someone else read it to me," Joe said gleefully.

Tracy takes the letter, and begins to read—

Dear Mr. Sherman,

It is with great enthusiasm, that I proudly announce a partnering between R&R Industries Inc. and inventor Joseph A. Sherman.

The (company) will enter into a long-term negotiation agreement with Mr. Sherman allowing for the licensing regarding: "The Thrust Enabling Objective System," United States Patent Number US9,534,540B2 issued January 3rd, 2017.

The actual terms and conditions of the licensing agreement will be discussed by (company) representatives at a time and date of their choosing. We at the (company) feel confident that this amalgamation between R&R Industries, Inc.(company) and Joseph A. Sherman (inventor) will be both beneficial and profitable to all parties involved.

We will contact you setting the time, date, and place where said negotiations are to be held as attended by both parties and their representatives.

Again, our hardy congratulations, as we look forward to entering into this joint business venture.

Most Respectfully,
Jonathan Samuels
Vice President of New Product
Research and Development R&R Industries, Inc.

"Wow, Joe! That certainly sounds like a bonafide offer by R&R Industries to develop your invention."

"Yeah, I truly think so," Joe answers confidently. "Hey, what's for dinner tonight, babe?"

"One of your favorites; brisket and egg noodles!" Tracy calling it out like a waitress placing a dinner order to a cook in the kitchen. Tracy makes a quick dash to the cased opening dividing the kitchen from the living room. "Josh, Laura, I'll be serving dinner in about 15 minutes, be here!" Tracy barks out the order like an army drill sergeant. Tracy turns around returning to the oven to check on the brisket.

"What's the occasion?" Joe asked inquisitively. "No occasion, decided to serve you a meal you haven't had for a while," Tracy humbly replied.

"I just developed one hell of an appetite!" as Joe scoots his chair closer to the kitchen table getting ready for a meal fit for a king.

"Thanks, honey." Joe proudly smiles with gleam in his eyes.

"You're welcome, honey. Kids dinner is being served," Tracy commands Josh and Laura to come into the kitchen taking their normal seating positions at the table. "Here, let's eat before the food gets cold," Tracy confirms with a smile as she sits next to Joe's right.

"Hey guys, got some great news to share with you after dinner, you're going to love it," Joe looking at Josh and Laura, then gets back to eating dinner.

One year later, at R&R Industries, Joseph A. Sherman, 48, five-foot-six, black hair with just a hint of grey highlights, always with a look as if he's deep in thought. Joe has been unwillingly initiated to be the pivotal point in the most rigorist research and development schedule he has very been subject to; now compelled to completing the project mandated by company guidelines.

"Joe, did you see the changes that the boys in the propulsions lab came up with?" alerted Ryan Comfort, Senior Chief Engineer, 43, thin build, brown hair with a slight receding hairline, sporting a pair of tinted prescription aviator glasses.

"Yeah, I just saw the report," Joe reluctantly answered. "So how much of the design are these guys going to change?"

"The change involves where the air inlet doors will be located around the mid-engine nacelle just in front of the air injection unit. They think relocating the doors slightly will improve transition time when the (A.I.U.) starts up to draw air in."

"Okay, no big deal," shrugs Joe looking at Ryan. "I knew from way back that something would have to change sooner or later."

"I'll tell you this Joe, all the engineers are really impressed with your design."

As Ryan praised Joe on his design savvy, just then, Sheryl Davis, working in the programming lab approaches Joe and Ryan to share some important news with them.

"Hi guys," as Sheryl stopped where Joe and Ryan were standing. "Did you hear, we're getting an unexpected visit from some of Uncle Sam's people? The only thing we've been told is that government personnel from Homeland Security will be spending a couple of days at the facility. No one knows why they're coming."

Ryan turns to Sheryl, thanking her for the heads-up. She then walks back to the programming lab. Joe turns to Ryan with a very concerned look on his face asking, "Why are these guys coming here? What do they have to do with my system?"

"I don't know, Joe. We didn't get much advanced warning that they were coming," Ryan exclaimed with uncertainty. "I do know that we have to stay out of their way. Not get involved with anything they're working on."

Joe tries to validate an answer from Ryan by exclaiming, "I didn't think that Homeland Security would have anything to do with my invention?"

Ryan counters Joe's point with, "I agree with you, Joe; maybe they just want to get familiar with your system. They may have other applications for T.E.O.S."

"Okay, Ryan," as Joe backs down from his flurry of inquisitions. "You probably have had more experience dealing with these government types. I hope they leave my system alone; not trying to change anything."

After all the scuttlebutt that was circulating around the company, about a surprise visit from government operatives, Homeland Security, and the defense department, finally came to the light of reality, an entourage of government personnel arrive at R&R Industries, on a bright, fateful Friday morning. They are led by a United States Army colonel as they marched in precision military unison down the hallway. Zak Taylor, human resources representative, guided the colonel's group to the auditorium in the main building. Minutes later, an announcement over the company P.A. system instructed anyone currently involved with the T.E.O.S. project to attend a meeting being held in the main auditorium. The U.S. Army colonel walked over to the podium, adjusted both right and left microphones, then cleared his throat before speaking, "Good morning, ladies and gentlemen, my name is U.S. Army Colonel Jim Thayer, I will be in charge of the team assigned to the T.E.O.S. project. I ask that anyone not affiliated with our team stay away from the electronics and integration lab for the next couple of days. We will be performing in depth studies of the complete system using a variety of simulation parameters. This will determine the trustworthiness of the system, should we decide to use it for military applications."

"Excuse me, Colonel, my name is Joe Sherman, I'm the inventor of T.E.O.S," Joe raising his hand so he could be noticed.

"Yes, Mr. Sherman, I'm aware of who you are," as the colonel stared straight at Joe. "There is no need for concern. We just want to make sure that the system can deliver. Now if you will excuse me, my team and I have much to do, not much time to do it in. Thank you to everyone here for their cooperation."

After Colonel Thayer left the auditorium with his team of operatives, Joe turns to Ryan with a smirk indicating that Joe was not at all convinced of the Colonel's sincerity towards non-interference with T.E.O.S. "I just don't know, Ryan," as Joe expresses his feelings with great uncertainty. "I haven't had a whole lot of experience with these military types, so it's hard for me to read them."

As Ryan looks at Joe, he flashes a smile, then proceeds to explain to Joe what he has learned about these military types, "Don't concern yourself too much with what they say; it's what they don't say but do that should always be the apprehension regarding their actions."

Joe looking at Ryan, shakes his head in disbelief. "I guess that would make sense. If we're not one of them, why should they tell us anything."

Ryan continues as he gives the perfect example of denial and misinformation that the government and military are so well known for.

Ryan begins to outline how the United States Air Force established a department whose function was to keep track, recording every encounter of unidentified flying objects. Most of these sightings would be documented and mostly debunked by the Air Force as overactive imaginations by those that said that they saw something in the night sky. Other accounts witnessed by the public would be dispelled as merely some kind of weather balloon, clouds, stars, or commercial airliner whose lights or reflective surfaces contributed to an abnormal profile resembling a UFO. For years, the cover up and charade generated by those within the Air Force's "Project Blue Book" continued to confuse and deceive the public into believing that there was always a logical explanation for what the public thought they saw. Luckily, many other organizations after the United States Air Force discontinued "Project Blue Book" in 1969, the continued interest and fascination regarding unidentified flying objectives was not a subject that would randomly be dispersed from the minds of those convinced that something unexplainable was out there. Ryan continues to elaborate that the military, for the sake of public interest and preventing mass hysteria, felt such information should not become readily accessible. We are now in the same predicament at R&R Industries. Government operatives have come in to learn everything about T.E.O.S. They will dissect the system piece by piece until they're convicted there is a way to control it if they had to.

"Jeez, what a pisser," as Joe massages the back of his neck, as if trying to relieve a bad neck ache. "Well, I certainly got one hell of a social science lesson on what these government types will stoop to in order to get what they're after."

Ryan comments by saying, "I can't believe that the United States government would do anything to jeopardize the safety of hundreds or thousands of commercial airliners that fly the skies every day. I just got a weird thought that crossed my mind. What if the United States government wanted to use this as some kind of anti-terrorist weapon; they could control being able to bring any plane down that they wanted because of suspected terrorist actions?"

"Oh my God," shouted Joe. "The ultimate doomsday scenario that would kill the terrorists, yet leave the United States government blameless."

"No, I can't believe our own government would be so cruel and heartless to kill a plane load of people just to stop a few terrorists," Joe cried out in sheer terror.

"I don't know about you, Ryan, but I'm going to keep my thoughts in deep reservation," as Joe became pensive after making his personal declaration.

"Listen, Joe, we may be wet behind the ears assuming that the government will use your invention to take out planes that become a threat," as Ryan reassured Joe of their faulted and twisted logic towards the government.

"I hear you, my friend, we can only hope that both of us are absolutely wrong. That my invention will be used only to save lives, not take them away."

"Hey, Joe, should we go see the boys in the propulsions lab to see exactly what their beef is about the air inlet doors?"

"Sure," Joe agreed instantly to Ryan's request. "Let's turn an almost-lousy day into something more constructive," as Joe places his left hand on Ryan's right shoulder, as they head down the hallway to the propulsions lab.

It's been rough for Joe traveling back and forth over the last year from home to R&R Industries. All in a grand effort to finish up the T.E.O.S. project on schedule; unless a glitch or two pop up at the last moment, like the propulsion boys getting a weird hair up their butts deciding to make a minor mod as the project is nearing completion. After Joe and Ryan resolve the issue with the air inlet doors, Joe decides enough is enough for one day. Turning to Ryan, Joe lets out a sigh saying, "Okay, that's it for me. I'm heading back to the hotel, get into the shower take all this bad stigma off me."

"Sounds like a good idea, Joe. I'm going to wrap up my day in a few, then head home myself. I'll see in the morning."

"Ryan, want me to bring some donuts?"

"Yeah, sounds great Joe. Don't forget; I like jelly filled!"

"You and I both. Just have the coffee ready to go when I get in."

"That's a deal, Joe."

"Good night, Ryan."

"Good night, Joe."

Joe grabs his briefcase walking down the hallway towards the main elevators. Joe arrives back at the hotel, swipes his room card, opening the door as he flings his briefcase on the adjacent single bed. Joe takes out his cell phone, as he presses the quick dial button for home. He stands by the window looking over the skyline, as he waits for Tracy to pick up. "Good evening, honey. Just got into my hotel room. The boys in the propulsions lab had a change to the location of the air inlet doors around the outside of the mid-engine nacelle."

Tracy interrupts, quickly preventing Joe from going on to a lengthy and mechanical engineering explanation that would surely leave her dumbfounded.

"Oh, I'm sorry, honey, I get carried away sometimes."

"It's okay," says Tracy. "You engineering types have to explain everything in the most minute details."

"Yeah, you're right about that," Joe boastfully agreeing. "But, seriously, I may have to be here a couple more days until the engineers finish testing the air injection unit with the new location for the air inlet doors. I was told they should be able to wrap this all up in a couple of more months. They feel confident that the system will perform flawlessly when the prototype is installed on one of their jet engines. Got to go, babe, I'm tired; still have to eat dinner and shower. I'll try to get some answers on how much longer I will need to be here, or if I can take a break so I can come home to see you and the kids."

"I love you," as Tracy affirms her unwavering commitment to Joe. "Don't worry about when you can come home. It's imperative that the project continue on its scheduled time frame. You don't want to get the one that gives you a paycheck to get upset with you."

"No, that would not be good right now," as Joe assesses his duties towards R&R Industries, "Let me go, I love you and give the kids a big hug and kiss from me."

"I will," assuring Joe that everything will be fine. "Good night, Joe."

"Good night, Tracy, call you tomorrow night."

Chapter 3

It's been a grueling three months for Joe along with the whole staff of engineers and designers as they make preparations to finish up the T.E.O.S. project right on schedule. Joe and Ryan busily discuss last minute tweaks on the preliminary test systems that will be mounted onto an experimental aircraft R&R Industries plans to use for the maiden flight. "Ryan is the Airbus 320 being used for the test flight going to have only one T.E.O.S. system installed?" as Joe inquires.

"Yeah, Joe, we decided it would be better to have only one engine carry a test system," Ryan continues to explain to Joe, in more detail, the reason for the decision. "Most of the system engineers have all agreed that the chance of a system wide cascade failure could be greatly reduced by having only one system onboard. Since none of us are exactly sure how the system may react by having multiple systems, it is best that, for now, we keep it limited, lessening the chances of either mechanical instability or electrical feedback, compromising the integrity of only one system while leaving other systems unaffected. After getting all the test data compiled, we can review it more objectively, making certain that all systems onboard the aircraft will work synchronously, and still be independent from one another. The most important reason for the decision is that should we mount two systems onboard, one for each engine, if there was some sort of catastrophic failure, and let's assume that both systems closed off the shielding blade assemblies, creating dual engine stall, unavoidably leaving the aircraft with no thrust to maintain lift. All those onboard would be doomed to die. So as an extreme safety precaution it was voted that one was the best alternative for this test flight."

After Ryan's explanation to Joe about the specifics regarding the test flight of the system, Joe just looked down for a moment, shaking his head as he fathomed in his mind the shear devastation of what would happen if the systems negatively interacted with each other. It was so somber of a thought that Joe decided to take a wild gamble to lighten the mood after such a realistic peek into uncertain disaster. "Yeah Ryan, I agree. It wouldn't be a good thing if the inventor of T.E.O.S. goes down with his own creation," as Joe looks at Ryan, laughs, then with a grimace expression, conceding that truth is greater than fiction.

Ryan looking right at Joe then asks, "You want to be onboard when we take it up for the first time?"

Joe proudly replying, "Are you kidding, Ryan? I have to be on that flight so the world can see that even the inventor can feel safe with his system, so should everyone else."

Ryan answers Joe's statement saying, "Okay, Joe, we'll let you know on what day the flight will take place. Don't be late! We'll have to leave without you," Ryan producing a big smirk on his face.

"I'll be there, Ryan. I wouldn't miss this for all the tea in China. I'm going back to the hotel room, pack my bags, get ready for the trip back home."

"Thanks, Joe! For all your help. Not to mention all the useful input during the early and later development stages of T.E.O.S." As Ryan shakes Joe hand placing his left hand on Joe's right upper shoulder.

Joe returning to his hotel room, takes his cell phone out of his pants' left pocket, as he speed dials the home number. After three rings, Tracy answers. "Hi honey, how are you doin', babe?"

Tracy, "I'm doin' good, how are things at R&R?"

Joe, "I believe we're at a point in the development of the system where they won't need me anymore. I have a scheduled flight back home in the morning. I'll be able to spend some much well-deserved time with you and the kids."

Tracy, "That's great, Joe, I'm glad you're coming home to be with us for a while."

Joe, "I asked Ryan to make sure to let me know when the test flight is to be scheduled. I don't even know where it's going to take place," as Joe confirms to Tracy the future events happenings with the project. "I did ask Ryan that he make certain that I was informed in regards to when the test flight would take place. I need to be there; I need to be on that aircraft when it takes off," as Joe adamantly defenses his convictions on the matter. "Honey, let me go. I'll see you and the kids tomorrow when I get in. I'm glad I was able to book a Saturday flight back so I can spend time with you and the kids as soon as I get in," as Joe happily announces his weekend intention for his family.

Tracy, "Okay, good night, Joe. Call me when you land at the airport. I want to make sure that the kids are around when you come home."

"I will," Joe confirms Tracy's wishes.

Tracy, "Good night, honey."

Joe, "Good night, babe, see you all tomorrow."

Two weeks after Joe is home, with plenty of time to spend with Tracy, Josh, and Laura, a call comes in from Ryan Comfort. As Joe picks up the home phone, he presses the answer button saying, "Hey there, Ryan, how the heck are you?"

Surprised by Joe's salutation, Ryan asks, "How did you know it was me?"

Joe replies, "I had a feeling it might be you. I figured a week, maybe two, you boys would have everything in place to ready the test flight on T.E.O.S. Not to mention that the number that I saw on the handset display is the extension number in your office."

"That was pretty good, Joe," Ryan complimenting Joe's mental acuity associating people to their phone numbers. "Okay, Joe, are you ready? Everything will be ready to go in about a week."

"Where is this going to take place," inquires Joe.

"You're going to love this one. Upper management decided to hangar the A320 used for the test flight at Roswell International Air Center, in New Mexico."

"*What!* That's incredible," Joe beaming a broad smile. "Why Roswell, of all places?" Joe asking in a curious manner.

Ryan replies, "Some of the top executives have gotten a glimpse of T.E.O.S., thinking that it was exotic and complex-looking enough that Roswell would provide a proper backdrop for such an advanced prototype."

"Man, I'm impressed," exclaims Joe.

"I'll send you all the details in an encrypted email. See you, Joe."

"See you Ryan," as Joe hangs up the phone.

Beautiful autumn day, winds ten to fifteen miles per hours from the northwest, scattered clouds, with just a nip of cool in the air. There was a certain excitement and electricity emanating from all those participating on the morning where an aviation first would be historically documented, as T.E.O.S. had its first monumental and uncompromised, successful flight. Invited representatives from local TV and newspapers were on hand to interview the countless scores of technicians, engineers, along with test pilots chosen to take up the altered bird on its maiden flight. An Airbus A320 is towed out from experimental hangar number ten; as designated by R&R Industries at Roswell International Air Center, New Mexico. After years of research and development, the once unprecedented idea had finally turned into a reality. Now the maiden flight of T.E.O.S. would indisputably make the history books. Joe arrives at Roswell International Air Center, then shuttles to where the T.E.O.S.-equipped A320 is ready for test flight. Joe arrives at where the A320 is—outside hangar ten—with technicians and engineers going over final preparations before the flight. Joe steps off the shuttle, walking over to the A320 as he is met by Ryan Comfort who is overseeing all visual and mechanical inspections prior to takeoff. Joe confirms, "I was not going to miss this. Thanks for letting me know so I can be part of this historic moment."

"Anytime, my friend. R&R Industries wants you here to witness the maiden flight, everyone at R&R wants it to succeed. It's all of our futures if the system does what it is supposed to do," as Ryan assures Joe of his importance towards the project.

"Okay, Ryan. I have to ask. Whose idea was it for the paint job on the A320?"

"Why? Don't you like the color scheme?" Ryan sounding surprised on why Joe was asking. "Red, orange, and yellow pin striping along the fuselage then curving up to the top of the rudder stab?"

"Mm, I had a motorcycle that I once disassembled, then had all the plastic body parts and gas tank painted. The color scheme is something I did many years back. I decided to repaint my 1976 Kawasaki KZ650 at my father's diesel shop. I applied red, orange, and yellow pin striping to accent the tank, side covers, and duck tail."

Ryan succumbing to the truth, "I have a confession to make. I called your wife; asked her what your favorite color scheme was? She told me about that motorcycle you re-did. I got management's permission to paint the A320 with the special color scheme. Did you notice, even has *T.E.O.S. Equipped* stenciled on the one outboard engine where the system is mounted. If we are going to advertise, then let's advertise!"

As Joe shakes Ryan's hand, "Thank you, my friend. I'm very honored with what you did. Now I definitely need to be onboard."

Moments away from the maiden flight of the T.E.O.S. Equipped Airbus A320. Crew, along with invited technical personnel, select members of the media are eagerly waiting take-off. "Hey Ryan, so if today is a complete success, what's the next stage?" Joe asks anxiously as he is buckling his seat belt.

"The next stage is; R&R will start looking for contractors so we can outsource the parts and assemblies," Ryan replies to Joe's questioning.

"Hey! are you guys going to use only parts made in the U.S.A.? We need to keep it in the family," Joe inquires.

"We are certainly going to shoot for that, Joe," Ryan confirms.

"*Great!* Remember, I'm just a phone call away. Need anything from me, I'm here for you guys," Joe eagerly showing his support.

Ryan acknowledges with, "I know that, Joe. Thanks!"

Everyone that's to be on the A320 test flight is now aboard, buckled in awaiting takeoff. In the cockpit, the captain radios into the tower requesting clearance for takeoff. "Tower, this is A320 TEOS1" (*designator given to the test A320*) "requesting clearance for take-off. Will turn to a heading of two-three-five degrees, activating T.E.O.S. test engine one as directed by R&R Industries in- flight technicians."

"Roger, A320 TEOS1 you have clearance for take-off, runway three. Wind's currently ten miles per hours, coming out from the northwest."

"Roger, cleared for take-off, runway three, A320 TEOS1 proceeding." The Airbus A320 accelerates down the runway, rotates making a perfect take off. After thirty minutes in the air, all final system checks are completed, Air Traffic Control is informed that flight maneuvers with the activated T.E.O.S. system are about to begin. R&R Technician 1, Chris Potter, is heard over the inboard intercom system, "Initiating system test ALPHA, opening Air Intake Doors. Air Injection Unit start up. Impeller unit to full rotational parameters. System test BETA, Shielding Blade Assembly, closed."

R&R Technician 2, Max Seneca is heard over the onboard intercom, "N1 rotational speed at turbofan at 50% of nominal. N2 rotational speed holding steady at 45-47% of nominal. No significant increase in Turbine Gas Temperature (TGT) and Exhaust Gas Temperature values (EGT)."

Senior R&R System Technician Sam Diamond calls to the cockpit giving instructions to the flight crew, "Captain, increase to three quarter throttle, perform sharp bank to starboard, decreasing forward air speed, determine any unusual drop in performance."

Captain replies, "Roger that, initiating maneuver."

Again, Max is heard over the onboard intercom, "N1 rotational speed at turbofan increased to 58% of nominal. N2 rotational speed holding steady at 51% of nominal. No significant increase in TGT and EGT values."

Sam calls to the cockpit instructing the captain, "Captain, perform emergency climb maneuver, increase climb rate, twenty-five hundred feet per minute, hold for five minutes, maintain present heading."

Captain replies, "Roger that, initiating maneuver, on my mark."

Max calls out test results over the onboard intercom, "N1 rotational speed at turbofan decreased to 42% of nominal. N2 rotational speed holding steady at 49% of nominal. No significant increase in TGT and EGT values."

As Joe turns to look at Ryan, he has produced the biggest boyish grin as he mentions one of his most important findings during the whole test flight, "Hey, Ryan! Would you believe it. I haven't soiled my underwear yet! I'm impressed."

Ryan looks at Joe with a very disturbed expression stating, "You would be a big disappointment flying with the Blue Angels or the Thunderbirds."

Joe raises both his arms saying, "Hey! I just came up with the idea. I never said that I would be performing any kind of crazy stunts to test them."

Sam calls into the cockpit to inform the captain, "Captain, all planned test maneuver results have been plotted and recorded. You may return to Roswell when ready."

"Roger that, plotting reciprocal course to Roswell International Air Center. ETA, 35 minutes."

Captain radios Tower, "Requesting landing clearance for Roswell, A320 TEOS1."

Tower replies, "A320 TEOS1 you are cleared to land, runway two-one, winds from the west, northwest at 10 mph."

Captain, "Roger tower, A320 TEOS1 heavy inbound and clear."

Twenty miles out from the airport, Chris Potter notices a red blinking light on his control console. He immediately alerts Sam Diamond, that a blinking red warning light just lit up, with no explanation on why. Sam unbuckles his seat belt as he approaches the control console in question. Sam asks Chris if he can determine where the fault may be coming from. "I'm not sure, sir. I was casually watching the

42

console when I noticed that the red light on the panel started to blink."

"Can you think of anything that would generate a fault causing the warning light to activate?" asked Sam showing concern.

"No, I don't have an explanation for this anomaly." As Chris answers with a baffled look as he directly stared at Sam standing over him.

"Okay, keep a close eye on your console. Any change, any change at all, let me know immediately. We may need to get the system engineers involved on this quick."

As Sam returns to his seat, he feels someone grab his arm, it was Ryan Comfort. "Sam, what's going on up there?"

Sam, "We got a red blinking light on console 1, Ryan. We're not too far from the airport, we should be alright until then."

Ryan, "Keep me informed should anything else changes, Sam."

"I will, Ryan," Sam heads back to his seat buckling his seat belt.

As Chris surveys his control console, he notices that the red blinking light has increased in frequency causing the light to blink at a faster rate. Chris recalls Sam back out to control console 1. Chris was being very discreet on not announcing anything about the blinking light out loud so others in the cabin would not be alerted that something may be wrong. Sam again approaches control console 1 noticing that the frequency of the red light has increased its rate of blinking. Just then, the sound of electric motors begins to whine from the T.E.O.S. test unit. Chris gets a confirmation from his console that the shielding blade assembly is closing, preventing air from reaching the engine intake. Ryan immediately leans his head to the right as he looks down the aisle to where Sam is standing at console 1. After the intake is completely closed off, the whine of the T.E.O.S. engine begins to decrease in speed. The A320 captain calls over the onboard intercom that T.E.O.S. engine has stalled, all attempts for restart have failed. Sam calls the cockpit to ask the captain on the condition of the T.E.O.S. test engine, "Captain, what is our engine status as of right now?"

Captain replies, "We still have power and thrust to engine number 2. T.E.O.S. engine 1 has zero power, no thrust. It's a dead engine."

Sam asks, "Can we make it back safely with only one engine?"

"No problem, replies the captain. This would not be the first time that I have had to fly with only one engine."

"How are all the other avionics doing?"

"They're doing fine. Everything is nominal, with no other systems in question, except for engine 1," informs the captain.

"What is our present ETA?" asks Sam.

Captain replies, "Should be landing in about five minutes."

"Great news. I'll make sure to spread the word in the cabin," as Sam replaces the microphone back on its holder. "Everyone, I just been informed by the captain that other than engine 1 being stalled, all other systems onboard are functioning correctly, we are less than five minutes from landing, the captain can get us down with only one engine being hot."

After the A320 landed safely back at Roswell International Center, as invited media, technicians, and engineers are deplaning, Sam steps up to the forward exit door, he spots Ryan Comfort with Joe Sherman already on the tarmac. He calls out to Ryan that he needs to talk to him about what happened while in the air with T.E.O.S. engine 1. Ryan and Joe wait while Sam makes it down the boarding stairs. Sam walks over to Ryan and Joe; he completes a circle of three as the men are standing face to face. "Ryan, when we get back to the shop, we got to find out what happened up there. Can't have a T.E.O.S. engine going berserk, deciding to shut down at thirty-eight thousand feet with a plane load of passengers."

"Okay, Sam" Ryan answers, "we'll go through all the test data to determine what went wrong."

The following week back from Roswell, early Monday morning, Ryan, Joe, and Sam reserve a conference room to look over all the flight test data on T.E.O.S. engine 1. All three men agreed that nothing in the flight test data could have possibly caused the engine to just shut down the way it did. Joe looks at both men saying, "William Shakespeare quoted it best in Macbeth, Act IV, Scene 1: *'Something wicked this way comes.'* I pray I'm wrong, but I hope that those military and government operatives that were at R&R Industries didn't booby-trap my system for some sick and sadistic reasons."

"Let's all hope not, Joe," Ryan expressing a faint glimmer of optimistic reasoning.

Chapter 4

Logo for television station, WFAA TV Channel, ABC in Dallas Texas.

"Good morning, everyone. I'm Rick Trauman."

And, "I'm Joanie Sable and this is the seven o'clock morning news."

Rick Trauman reporting, "It has now been two years since the massive move to design and build the latest jet engines with a brand-new technology called the Thrust Enabling Objective System."

Joanie Sable reporting, "This radically new safety improvement is the invention of one Joseph A. Sherman. It has taken years to develop and test. Using the latest in space-age technology and a watchful eye from R&R Industries, Inc. (one of the large jet engine manufacturers in the world) *photograph of the company headquarters shown on a green screen in the studio*, this system has been proven to be one of the most important safety apparatuses in the world of jet engine development today."

Rick Trauman reporting, "The simplicity of this new system is that it can be retrofitted on to older engines still in service by removing the forward nacelle (cowling where the intake is at), *as a photograph is shown on a green screen in the studio*, then replacing it with a new nacelle section that houses all the components needed to make the Thrust Enabling Objective System perform its job. Earlier last week, WFAA TV Channel 8, ABC sent Danielle Gomez to visit R&R Industries, Inc. to learn, in detail, from the people that helped develop it more about this incredible system."

Joanie Sable reporting, "WFAA TV Channel 8, ABC will be dispatching a film crew—cameraman Alex Simpkins along with field reporter Danielle Gomez—to Dallas-Fort Worth International Airport, to get mixed feelings and reactions from various passengers on the new improvements made to an Airbus A330 they will board this morning."

Both Danielle Gomez and cameraman Alex Simpkins arrive at Dallas-Fort Worth International Airport. After showing their station credentials they were allowed to pass onto the main concourse where a T.E.O.S.-equipped United Airlines Airbus A330 was to take off to Philadelphia. Danielle with cameraman Alex move their way over to the boarding gate where people are waiting to board United Airlines flight *1105*. One middle aged looking man is approached for an interview. "Excuse me, my name is Danielle Gomez, I'm a reporter with WFAA TV Channel 8, ABC from Dallas, Texas. Sir, may I have a moment of your time before you board your flight?"

Passenger, "Certainly, I got time before I board my flight."

Danielle, "First of all, sir, may I ask what seat you'll be sitting in?"

Passenger, "Sure, I'm seated in *21D*."

Danielle, "Sorry to ask, I just take down certain notes about a passenger, then I use their seat number to match my notes to that person."

Passenger, "No problem."

Danielle, "Sir, are you aware that the A330 you'll be flying is equipped with a system called T.E.O.S.?"

Passenger, "No, I wasn't aware. What does it do?"

Danielle, "Well, it's supposed to protect the engines if anything should fly into them."

Passenger, "No kidding."

Danielle, "I understand from the engineers that the system is very reliable."

Passenger, "*Great!* We can use all the help we can get so we make it down in one piece."

Danielle, "Thank you, sir, for your time. Have a nice flight," as she smiles at the passenger.

Passenger, "Thank you. I'm glad you told me about T.E.O.S. By the way, what does it stand for?"

Danielle, "Thrust Enabling Objective System."

Passenger, "Okay, not exactly sure I understand, but as long as it keeps us all safe, I'm good with it, thank you."

Danielle with cameraman Alex look around the United Airlines gate for someone else to interview. Danielle spots an older woman clutching her handbag, just looking as if she is in a daze. Danielle approaches the woman, as she stands to one side, "Ma'am, my name is Danielle Gomez, I'm with WFAA TV Channel 8, ABC from Dallas, Texas. May I have a moment of your time for a quick interview?"

Woman answers with a shaky and nervous voice, "Yes, that's fine."

Danielle, "First of all, ma'am, may I ask what seat are you sitting in?"

Woman, "I'm seated in *52A*."

Danielle, "Thank you, ma'am, this is just to correlate my notes with the people I'm interviewing. Did you know that the Airbus you'll be flying on is equipped with a revolutionary new system that is designed to protect its jet engines?"

Woman, "You have to forgive me dear. I get very nervous when I fly," woman passenger answering in a foreboding manner. "I'm aware that things can happen and there is nothing anyone of us can do to prevent it."

Danielle addressing the woman in a soothing voice, "Ma'am, I have been assured by the engineers that developed this system, that it will protect the engines from damage or destruction. With all the other existing systems that aircraft are equipped with, this is now a very, very safe aircraft to fly."

Woman, "Thank you, dear. It makes me feel a little better to know the airlines are doing everything they can to make air travel safer for people like me."

Danielle, "Have a great flight, ma'am. Please, don't be worried," Danielle lightly shakes the woman's right hand.

Woman, "Thank you so much, my dear. You have made me feel much better." Danielle smiles than turns walking away as she and cameraman Alex move to another part of the United Airlines gate.

Danielle approaches another passenger sitting at the United Airlines gate. As she gets closer, the passenger gets up, Danielle side steps in front of the woman that just got up, asking if she would submit to a quick interview. The woman abruptly answers, "I can't right now, young lady; I need to use the restroom quickly before I board my flight, maybe another time."

As Danielle side steps back, she assures the woman, "No problem, maybe another time." As the woman hurriedly strides to the women's restroom on the concourse as Alex is still shooting.

Danielle composed herself for the camera shot as Alex cues her that she's on. "Hello everyone, I thought I would get one last passenger before they boarded their flight. Regrettably, the call of nature was much more pressing. I'm going to turn this back over to you, Rick and Joanie. Reporting from Dallas-Fort Worth International Airport, this is Danielle Gomez, WFAA, TV Channel 8, ABC."

A clear and sunny morning as the last of the passengers board Lufthansa flight *1309* bound for Frankfurt, Germany, with a stopover at LaGuardia airport, NYC. As the last passenger walks the aerobridge from the west terminal gate *A*, flight crew prepared for the scheduled take off from Denver International Airport. Flight is being piloted by Captain Jerome Nudel and First Officer Hank Nisselsen. Forward exit door locked and secured from both sides. As the Airbus A340 rolls down the service apron, captain and first officer go through their final checklist prior to takeoff. Captain holds short of the runway to await clearance from the tower. Captain, "Requesting departure clearance, Lufthansa *1309*."

Tower, "Lufthansa *1309*, cleared for departure, runway three-five."

Captain, "Roger, cleared for departure runway three-five, Lufthansa *1309*, rolling."

Aircraft takes off, rotates, climbing to twenty-five hundred feet. Moments into the flight, the first officer notices a flock of birds flying towards the starboard side of the aircraft.

First Officer, "*Damn!* We got birds."

Captain gives the order to activate T.E.O.S. system, after system activates, several large thumps can be heard by crew and passengers. One passenger sees a bird smash into a starboard window near where he was seated.

Captain, "Tower, Lufthansa *1309*, bird strike!"

Tower, "Lufthansa *1309*, any damage to aircraft?"

Captain, "T.E.O.S. system activated, request return runway to Denver for visual on damage to engines and aircraft."

Tower, "Lufthansa *1309*, you are cleared to land on runway one-seven. Will you require emergency assistance?"

Captain, "Negative, will notify. Cleared to land, runway one-seven, Lufthansa *1309* clear." Aircraft lands, then instructed to proceed to service apron where waiting ground crews will inspect for any damage to engines or fuselage due to bird strike. After an hour, ground crews determine that other than dead birds laying just on the other side of the shielding blades, no birds entered the air intake of any of the four engines. Several dings and dents were apparent along the starboard side of the aircraft, also along the outer cowlings of the engines. T.E.O.S was successfully able to prevent major damage from happening to all engines. After dead birds were removed, aircraft was cleared by ground inspection crew to resume its scheduled flight. Take off of Lufthansa *1309* was successful, with no further incidents.

Details of the incident hit the news media, as an overwhelming response from air travelers along with the airline poured in from everywhere. *Logo for television station KTVD TV 20 Denver, Colorado.* "Good afternoon, welcome to the twelve o'clock news at noon. I'm Trevor Howard."

Camera scans. "I'm Cynthia Ashton, our top story; near disaster was averted this morning when a Lufthansa flight took off from Denver International Airport. Its destination was Frankfurt, Germany with a stopover at LaGuardia International Airport, NYC. As the aircraft was ascending to around twenty-five hundred feet, the aircraft was hit by a flock of mallards. Luckily, no damage to engines or aircraft occurred. We have been told that the engines were protected by a new onboard system called the Thrust Enabling Objective System. The system was activated while in flight, keeping all four engines from being severely damaged. We contacted our NYC TV affiliate WABC Channel 7 to interview passengers, as they continue on to Frankfurt, Germany.

"We now switch you over to WABC Channel 7 field reporter Alicia Rodriquez who is already at LaGuardia International Airport."

Alicia along with cameraman Chuck Stafford walk towards the Lufthansa Airlines gate to catch a couple of interviews with some of the passengers aboard the Lufthansa flight struck by a flock of birds as it took off this morning from Denver International Airport. Alicia approaches one of the passengers sitting and waiting. "Excuse me, sir. My name is Alicia Rodriquez with WABC

Channel 7 TV here in NYC. You were on Lufthansa flight *1309* when it was hit by a flock of birds, is that correct?"

"Yes," answered the passenger that was seated in *15H*. "Many of us heard several loud thumps of what sounded like something hitting the outside of the plane. I looked out over the right wing, saw a large bird skim across the window as it left a blood smear on the glass."

Alicia, "Sir, did you have any idea of what was going on?"

Passenger, "No, the captain never announced what was going on outside. I think that both the captain and first officer had their hands full at the time."

Alicia, "Does this change your thinking towards the safety of air travel?"

Passenger, "Yes," passenger nods his head, "I now feel more secure knowing that even the engines have a new level of safety that didn't existed before. You hear of planes going down because of severe engine damage."

Alicia, "Thank you for your time, sir. Have a safe flight to Frankfurt."

Passenger, "Thank you!"

Alicia proceeds to walk with her cameraman Chuck to another seating area at the Lufthansa gate to interview another passenger that was on flight *1309*.

Alicia, "Excuse me, sir. May I have a moment of your time? My name is Alicia Rodriquez with WABC Channel 7 TV here in NYC. I understand you were on-board the Lufthansa flight that was struck by a flock of birds on take-off at Denver International Airport?"

Passenger, "Yes, I was."

Alicia, "Did you see anything out your window that would have warned you of an impending bird strike?"

Passenger, "I was seated on the right side of the plane; seat *4K*, so I had a pretty good view out the window. I happened to look out the right window as I angled my view towards the front of the plane, I saw what looked like a flock of birds flying towards us."

Alicia, "How long after you saw the birds, did they hit the plane?"

Passenger, "Couldn't have been more than a minute; we heard thumping sounds as the birds were hitting the outside of the plane."

Alicia, "Did the captain ever make an announcement to what was going on?"

Passenger, "He might have been too busy to make an announcement."

Alicia, "Thank you, sir! I won't take anymore of your time, have a safe flight to Frankfurt."

Passenger, "Thank you. I enjoyed this interview."

"This is Alicia Rodriquez at LaGuardia International Airport, back to you in the studio."

WABC Studios, "Thank you, Alicia, for that informative report. In other news today…"

American Airlines flight *407* is towed back from the aerobridge as the flight crew begins startup sequence on the twin engines of the Airbus A319. A beautiful, crisp, fall evening for a routine flight from Newark Liberty International Airport to Chicago's O'Hare International Airport. Captain John Roberts and First Officer Larry Bergman at the controls. Aircraft taxis on to runway two-two for takeoff. As aircraft increases speed, then begins rotation, something is picked up off the runway hitting number 2 engine before T.E.O.S. system has a chance to complete activation.

Captain, "Tower, American *407* have picked up some kind of debris off runway."

Tower, "American *407*, any damage to engines or aircraft?"

Captain, "Not sure! T.E.O.S. system activated, but number 2 engine ingested debris off runway. Losing oil pressure and N1 rotational speed fast. This bird has one engine that's dying. Have no idea on the condition for the rest of the aircraft."

Tower, "Do you require emergency return clearance, American *407*?"

Captain, "That's affirmative, Tower."

Tower, "American *407*, you are cleared to land, runway two-two. Will have emergency vehicles standing by at end of runway two-two."

Captain, "Roger, clearance to land, runway two-two, American *407* out."

After American flight 407 lands safely with one powered engine, aircraft is instructed to proceed to a service apron where awaiting ground crews will inspect for damage to engines and fuselage due to runway debris. After an hour, inspection ground crews determine that the debris picked up off runway damaged engine number 2 only. Other than loose pieces of asphalt laying just on the outside of the shielding blades for number 1 engine, no debris entered the air intake. Rest of the aircraft was checked out for structural damage, several small dings and dents were apparent along the underside of the aircraft; also, on the front cowlings of each engine, the concentration of lifted debris was suspected due to suction pressure from both engines at takeoff. Regrettably, the aircraft still had one damaged engine and is grounded; placing it in an American Airlines hangar for closer inspection, and removal of the damaged number 2 engine.

Days later after the incident, the N.T.S.B. has an informal preliminary hearing in Washington D.C., on what caused American Flight *407* to lose an engine due to loosened chunks of asphalt sucked into engine number 2. Both Captain Roberts and First Officer Bergman were present, along with representatives from American Airlines, airport official, news media, along with aviation experts. The N.T.S.B. lead investigator responsible for the American flight *407* incident, Reginald (Reggie) Chandler, begins reading the incident report to all those present in the meeting hall. "Good morning, ladies and gentlemen. I want to assure everyone here that this is simply an informal hearing. Since there was no loss of lives just airline property, the purpose here is to determine exactly what occurred as the aircraft proceeded down the runway, thus picking up asphalt off the runway. I would like to ask Captain John Roberts for his testimony of what took place on the evening as the flight crew began their takeoff."

Captain Roberts, "Thank you, Mr. Chandler. My first officer Larry Bergman and I, proceeded to takeoff from Newark as we have done so many times before. Prior to rotating, thumps that sounded as if the plane was being pelted by large rocks could be heard clearly. We know for a fact that T.E.O.S. did activate automatically, but unfortunately the time differential from when the asphalt hit engine number 2 to when T.E.O.S. was fully activated was mere seconds. T.E.O.S. could not activate fast enough to protect engine 2 as it did protect engine 1."

Reginald Chandler, "Thank you, Captain Roberts."

Captain Roberts nods as he acknowledges.

Reginald Chandler, "First Officer Bergman, would you like to add to Captain Roberts testimony?"

First Officer Bergman, "Yes, I would, sir. First of all, I concur with everything Captain Roberts has told this N.T.S.B. panel. Second, I would like to express my eternal thanks to both the inventor and the aerospace engine company that developed the T.E.O.S. system. If not for T.E.O.S., we would have lost engine 1 as well, and would never have made it back to Newark so we could land safely while still having one good working engine. I have nothing more to add."

Reginald Chandler, "Thank you, First Officer Bergman."

"I'm sure that all of us here, realize that if not for the T.E.O.S. system, American flight *407* would have been a doomed flight, with all dead onboard. It is the conclusion of this N.T.S.B. panel that loosened chunks of asphalt from runway twenty-two were the cause of this near tragedy. The outcome could have been much worse as far as engine damage was concerned. Only the quick acting sensors around the front of each engine automatically activated the T.E.O.S system. The N.T.S.B. strongly feels that lack of proper runway repairs was the cause for the damage to the one engine. Failing infrastructure funds due to government cutbacks, kept that runway from being properly repaired and maintained. It is this panel's official recommendation to the F.A.A. that all runways at Newark Liberty International Airport be closely scrutinized for any sights of deterioration. Runways must endure the punishment of planes landing and taking off year-round, weather conditions from heat, cold, rain, snow, ice; all of which generate great stress on a surface that is the last earthbound platform before reaching for the sky and the first element that, with open arms, welcomes a plane with its passengers back to earth."

Chapter 5

A bitter cold and glooming day looms over Stockholm's Vasteras Airport as passengers prepare to board a Scandinavian Airlines flight *145* to Keflavik International Airport in Iceland, with a stopover in Kangerlussuaq Airport in Greenland. This flight will have a light passenger load since not many people are expected to travel to Iceland during this time of year. There have been reports coming in from Iceland that the Katla volcano has been showing signs of activity with random, minor eruptions almost every day. Many airlines in the northern part of Europe will continue their flights to parts of Greenland and Iceland. Until a major volcanic eruption occurs, there would be no cancelation of flights into the region for now. The last of the passengers have boarded, placing their carry-on luggage into the overhead storage compartments, locating their seats, buckling in, as they prepare for their flight. Forward exit door secured and locked, aircraft is towed as it backs away from the aerobridge. Tow bar disconnected; both of the engines have already been started by the flight crew. The crew consist of Captain Liam Eriksson along with First Officer William Hurst. The Airbus A321 stops short before taxiing onto the runway. Tower, "SAS *145* hold short, one heavy on final approach."

Captain, "Roger, will hold until cleared." After a Boeing B747 lands, Captain Eriksson is given take off clearance.

Tower, "SAS *145*, you are cleared for take-off, runway zero-one."

Captain, "Tower, clearance for take-off, runway zero-one, SAS *145*."

Tower, "SAS *145*, vector to leg Kangerlussuaq Greenland, good flight, tower out."

Captain, "Roger, tower, thank you, SAS *145*, we are clear and rolling."

SAS flight *145* throttles up, rotates, taking off then climbing to an altitude of thirty thousand feet.

"Sarah, I can't believe that you're still upset with me with what I said about that guy last night when we went to dinner at that restaurant *Lilla Ego*. I can't believe you, Jay, you made such a big deal about the guy coming over commenting on how nice I looked in my evening dress. You have to realize that if a man finds me attractive, that doesn't mean that I'm going to be so mesmerized that I'll get up from my chair, to run away with the guy. I just feel more of a woman when another man gives me such a compliment."

"I'm sorry, Sarah, I was just being a typical guy jumping the gun instead of thinking about it realizing that I have a beautiful woman; other men will find you just as beautiful and attractive as I do."

"Okay, Jay, I forgive you, but don't act like a jerk again."

"Yes, ma'am, thank you. Now the rest of the trip will not be a silent one-sided vacation."

SAS flight *145* completes its first leg, ready for approach at Kangerlussuaq airport in Greenland. There will be a two hour stop-over with the next leg from Greenland to Iceland being an estimated distance of about seven hundred fifty-six nautical miles. While flight *145* has been laid over in Greenland, there have been reports coming out of Iceland that the Katla volcano has had some minor eruptions, while no one at the Icelandic geological society can be certain when a major eruption will occur.

Almost two hours after the scheduled layover in Greenland, an announcement is heard coming over the airport public address system bringing concern to many of the passengers heading on to Iceland. Some of the closed-circuit monitors lining the concourse as well as the Scandinavian Airlines seating area are switched from airport flight information to latest news reports regarding further activity about Katla volcano in Iceland. Local news station Kalaallit Nunaata Radioa (KNR) is a public broadcasting company administered by the Greenlandic Government. They report that the Icelandic Geological Society has been providing station KNR with up-to-date seismic and geological data regarding the Katla volcano.

The IGS has issued warning for the small town of Hvolsvöllur, Iceland fearing that a magnitude 2.6 earthquake could cause minor but significant damage to such a small town. Already, some light tremors have been felt at about 1.0 on the Richter scale. No major eruptions have yet been recorded, but the area is still very unstable and unpredictable. What makes the Katla volcano so uncertain is that is lies underneath the Mýrdalsjökull glacier. It would not require an extremely violent eruption for the volcano to explode with enough force to completely break through melting most of the immense density of the glacier. Warnings have been issued to airlines and flight crews that will fly onto Iceland that they are to be vigilante, heeding all travel advisories should the Katla volcano unavoidably erupt, causing severe disruption to ground transportation along with atmospheric conditions not well suited for aircraft flying through the area.

After the two hour stop-over, along with travel alerts given about Katla volcano in Iceland, SAS flight *145* readies to depart on its final leg to Keflavík International airport in Iceland. Passengers re-board SAS *145*, the Airbus A321 is towed back from the aerobridge, engines have been started as the plane taxis while the crew performs a final takeoff checklist. Flight crew holds short of runway to await take off clearance from the tower. Captain, "Tower, SAS *145*, requesting take-off clearance."

Tower, "SAS *145* you are cleared for take-off, runway zero-nine."

Captain, "Roger, clearance for takeoff, runway zero-nine, SAS *145*."

Tower, "SAS 145, vector to Keflavik, Iceland, tower is clear."

Captain, "Thank you, tower, SAS *145*, we are clear and rolling."

Flight crew positioned the Airbus A321, applies brake, throttles up, proceeds down the runway, rotating, then taking off as it climbs to an altitude of thirty-five thousand feet.

The flight from Kangerlussuaq airport, Greenland to Keflavik-Reykjavík, Iceland is about two hours of flight time but with time differences between the two countries, the flight may seem longer. About 50 miles before reaching Keflavik-Reykjavik airport, the SAS *145* flight crew spots a large plume of dark smoke billowing upwards, immediately radioing in, to the Keflavik tower to verify of the Katla volcano eruption. Tower informs flight *145* that Katla volcano has erupted, spewing large amounts of ash into the air. They predict that the smoke column can reach an altitude of thirty-five to forty-five thousand feet. The width of the smoke column is estimated at about ten miles across, with prevailing winds from the south east; it is slowly moving towards Keflavik-Reykjavik Airport, Iceland.

There is no way to go around to avoid it. Fuel consumption estimates were only calculated with about a ten to fifteen percent reserve. Other airports in Iceland are too far, the plane does not have enough of a fuel reserve to travel to the farther airport destinations. After the crew discusses any and all possible options available to them, Captain and first officer make the swift decision to activate T.E.O.S. The flight crew will try to skim the outermost layer of the ash plume in an effort to lessen the fly-around distance required to clear the column of ash. The fuel reserves on hand should cover the deviation required to clear, then attempt to land using only Instrument Flight Rules since visibility will become extremely limited. The attention of some of the passengers was caught as they looked out of their left side window seats. They were in awe of the immense size of the ash plume as the flight crew precariously piloted their way around the smoke column without being enveloped in it. Captain, "Tower, SAS *145* on final approach. can you pick us up on radar?"

Tower, "SAS *145*, we have you on radar, we advise against trying to land. Visibility is limited to less than one quarter mile at times."

Captain, "No other choice. Fuel is running low, reserve almost gone, cannot reach any other airport, must land now."

Tower, "SAS *145*, you have clearance to land, runway zero-nine. Cross winds vary between 10-15 knots with medium gust at 25 knots."

Captain, "We are flying with T.E.O.S. activated; only way to get this bird down, without destroying both engines from volcanic ash ingestion."

Tower, "SAS *145*, twelve hundred feet, maintain glide slope, decrease speed to one hundred sixty knots, you should see runway less than one quarter of a mile."

Captain, "Wilco. Gear down and locked, we're lined up and ready to land." Captain Eriksson to First Officer, "Bill, give me fifteen degrees of flap."

First Officer, "Aye Captain, fifteen degrees of flaps."

Tower, "You're looking good, watch for crosswinds.' Good luck SAS *145*, tower clear."

Captain to First Officer, "Watch the attitude indicator, Bill, keep her straight."

First Officer, "I'll try, sir. These cross winds are a bitch!"

SAS *145* makes a successful landing at Keflavik-Reykjavik Airport, Iceland. Eventually, the ash cloud encompassed the airport, forcing all flights to be cancelled.

The day after the Katla volcano eruption, the SAS inspection crews were sent to inspect the aircraft closely for any visual signs of damages to engines and aircraft from the volcanic ash. The inspection crew reported into Scandinavian Airlines that the large amount of volcanic ash spewed as flight *145* was trying to land, had no effect on the engines or the exterior of the fuselage. The shielding blade assemblies on both engines were opened up and the inspection crew found no evidence of volcanic ash inside the intake of either engines. Other than a very heavy layer of ash still clinging to the plane's exterior, nothing more than a good washing would be required to get the aircraft back in service.

It's a warm, balmy morning in the beautiful city of Venice, Italy. Marco Polo Airport is bustling as passengers are busy getting to their airline counters, checking in their luggage, getting past the terminal security checkpoint, then settling in at their departure gates. Some of the passengers have a more adventurous agenda as they browse through all the duty-free shops hunting for unimaginable bargains and memorable keepsakes before returning back home with the proof that they were there having a good time, as they show friends and family. Over the P.A. system the announcement is made that passengers are to start boarding Qatar Airways flight *334* to Kuwait International Airport in Kuwait City. Qatar flight *334* is being piloted by veteran Captain Noor Kouri along with well-seasoned First Officer Asaad Shamoon. This will be a new experience for the captain and first officer. Both pilots have had a very short amount of hands-on to acclimate to simulator training for the Boeing

B787 Dream-liner which they are to pilot. Captain, "Tower, Qatar *334* requesting clearance for take-off."

Tower, "Qatar *334*, you have clearance for take-off, runway two-two."

Captain, "Roger, tower, clearance for take-off, runway two-two, Qatar *334*."

Tower, "Qatar *334*, have a good day and great flight."

Captain, "Thank you, tower, Qatar *334* is clear and rolling."

Captain to First Officer, "Okay Asaad, may Allah grant us a good flight."

Now for the long six hour and fifty-five minute, three thousand five hundred ninety-kilometer flight to Kuwait International Airport in Kuwait City.

"Ronnie, I overheard one of the passengers sitting a few seats down from us when we were in the departure lounge, I overheard that parts of the Middle East sometimes gets hit with a really bad dust storm called *Haboobs*. What would happen if one of those dust storms were to hit this plane on the way to Kuwait?"

"I wouldn't worry about it, Carmen. These storms are created by converging weather systems coming together as they start out in a thunderstorm. Down drafts force a column of air as it hits the ground, pushing large amounts of dust and debris into the air ahead of the thunderstorm. Then that downdraft becomes the forward gust that will travel as a gigantic wall of dust and debris moves over everything in its way."

"Ronnie, you don't think we would run into one of those *Haboobs* while we're on vacation in the Middle East, right?"

"Honey, I can't predict if we would get hit by a *Haboob* while in the Middle East."

Look, if there was one coming while in the air, I'm sure that the captain and first officer will do everything possible to avoid it and make sure that the passengers, and crew would not be injured or killed."

"So, I guess it can happen at any time and no one can stop it right, Ronnie?"

"No, Carmen, that's nature. No one controls nature. Look, even back home, there are severe dust storms in the Midwest. So, if we're ever in the Midwest we could be hit by a dust storm or a *Haboob*. Different names, same effect."

"Okay, Ronnie, I feel better after you explained all that to me."

"Carmen, lets enjoy the rest of our vacation, don't worry."

Only forty minutes left before landing at Kuwait International Airport. Air Traffic Control meteorologist reports a severe dust storm (*Haboob*) approaching Kuwait City from the west heading toward the Persian Gulf. The problem is whether the Qatar Airways flight will be able to reach the safety of the airport, safely land before the storm makes it impossible to see and land.

The captain gathers all necessary information from the ATC meteorologist to decide whether they should take a chance landing, to beat the storm in. The airplane has more than enough fuel reserves to be diverted to another airport, but the way the storm is heading, the flight could end up right in the middle of it. Captain, "Tower, watching radar, very worried that dust storm will intercept us before we have a chance to land."

Tower, "Because of the size of the storm, we can divert you to the nearest airport from here but we can't assume that the storm will not catch up quickly to overtake you as well."

Captain, "Tower, as the old American saying goes: *'Damned if you do, damned if you don't.'* We have to take our chances. So close to the airport, can't risk getting into a worst situation by flying to another airport. My first officer and I will ride this one out, do the best we can for the passengers and crew."

Back in the aircraft cabin, some of the passengers sitting on the left side of the plane look out their windows to notice what seems to be a giant wall of dust. It's still a distance away, but still moving east to where it will engulf Kuwait City. As Carmen Havasta, seated in *14A* looks out the left side window, her jaw just about drops as she nudges her husband Ronnie in seat *14B* to get his full attention. "Yeah Carmen, what do you need?"

"Ronnie, remember a while ago, I was asking you about those giant dust storm they call *Haboobs*?"

"Yes, how can I forget."

"Well, look out the window and tell me if what you see is one of those *Haboobs*?"

Ronnie leans over to get a better look out of Carmen's window. He focuses and replies as he looks at her, "Yeah, that's a *Haboob*, heading this way."

"So now what?"

Ronnie answers, "These pilots are trained for those type of storms. I noticed when we got on board, I looked in the cockpit and saw them. They both look Middle Eastern, or could be Kuwaiti. Stop worrying about it. I'm sure these pilots are trained to deal with this."

Back in the cockpit, captain Kouri mentions to his first officer, this will make driving and walking the city streets impossible unless everyone is wearing a full-face respirator. Even to be able to see where you're going would be nearly impossible as the dust will be so dense that it will block out the sun, turning the day into night. Aircraft of any kind would, of course, not be allowed to land or take off. The danger from massive amounts of dust would immediately consume jet engines and prop engines with enough dust to stall them if they dare to oppose the mighty *Haboob*.

Captain to First Officer, "Asaad, set the flaps, put the gear down, activate T.E.O.S., be ready to make quick corrections when we're in the storm. It may get rough, we got to get down!"

First Officer, in a light but apprehensive voice, "You know I am right, Captain. Allah likes us."

Captain, in an anxious and foreboding voice, "I hope Allah also likes the passengers and crew." The captain and first officer line up the aircraft as they spot the runway about one-quarter mile away. As the outer fringes of the storm begin to buffet the plane.

Captain and First Officer fight to maintain control, try keeping plane true to course. As they near the runway, a second squall, much heavier than the first causes the airplane to yaw and twist to the left.

Captain, in the same foreboding voice as before, "Asaad! watch the attitude indicator, we got to correct the rate of yaw on the plane. We will end up completely off the runway."

First Officer, "I'm sorry, Captain, the stick is hard to control, watching the attitude indicator to make sure we are on the glide slope and flying level."

Captain, "I know it's hard, Asaad, we're losing visibility fast and we have another 200 feet before we land. Watch your instruments and let's keep it straight."

Finally, the flight crew manages to land the plane realizing that they were maybe a couple of feet away from landing in the soft sand just to the left of the runway. Miraculously, it was an incredible landing considering the odds against the crew with very low visibility, strong cross winds trying to push the plane off the runway. Captain, "Asaad! Did you notice how close we came to running off the runway?"

First Officer, in a confident and joyous voice, "I knew Allah would protect us. I was never in doubt."

Captain, in a joking, but thankful voice, "Remind me to ask for you, next time we have to fly through a *Haboob*. I will feel so much better knowing that I have a lucky omen that can whisper in Allah's ear and he will listen."

Chapter 6

It's now been a couple of years since the last incident where T.E.O.S. was required to be deployed as a last lifesaving resort. John F. Kennedy International Airport, early spring evening, passengers are called by group to board Delta Airlines flight *4502* bound for Dublin, Ireland. Many passengers are ecstatic because in a couple of days it will be Saint Patrick's Day. Many of those onboard are the sons and daughters of immigrants that came from Ireland. Passengers have boarded; forward exit door secured and locked; aircraft is towed back from the aerobridge; pilots have started both engines, are now heading for the side apron, to wait for take-off clearance. A Boeing 777-200 is well packed for the long haul across the Atlantic before reaching the golden isle of Ireland. The Delta flight *4502* is being piloted by Gregg Deland, a retired United States Air Force Captain, whose missions included better than nine thousand flight hours in a Lockheed C130J Super Hercules.

First Officer Jerry Lopez is fairly new to the world of airline flying with just over three years employed by Delta Airlines. Captain, "Tower, requesting clearance for take-off, Delta *4502*."

Tower, "Delta *4502*, you are cleared for departure, runway three-one."

Captain, "Roger, tower, clearance for departure, runway three-one, Delta 4502."

Captain to First Officer Lopez, "Okay, Jerry, let's make this bird sing."

First Officer, "Aye, Captain."

Captain, "Tower, Delta *4502*, rolling, we are clear."

Aircraft takes off, rotates, then instructed to climb to thirty-seven thousand feet with course vector to a heading of five-zero point one-nine degrees. Aircraft now heading over the Atlantic Ocean on its way to Dublin.

Meanwhile in the cabin section of the Boeing 777, flight attendants prepare food and refreshments to be served during the long seven-plus hour flight to Ireland. Over in the Delta comfort plus seats *32D*, *32E*, *32F*, and *32G*, four young olive-skinned men are busily huddled close together speaking in their native tongue. One of the young men, Hayyan, seated in *32E* seat in-between the other three men, speaks to all of them, "I will get my backpack, go use one of the lavatories behind us; I will get our weapons ready so we can rush the cockpit when the time is right."

Sitting just to Hayyan's left, Salem asks, "Hayyan, do you think this will work?"

Hayyan, "We have practiced this many, many times. It will work, just be ready to take your positions as we rehearsed." Hayyan turning to his right to face Suske, sitting in seat *32F*, asking, "Suske, are you good with this? Joram, are you good with this?" as Hayyan turns back to his left, "Salem, are you good with this?"

All three men looking at Hayyan each answer, "Yes, Hayyan, we understand."

Hayyan, "Good, I'm counting on my brothers to make this happen. Be ready, you will know when."

An announcement is made that food and refreshments will be served as soon as the aircraft reaches its cruising altitude, within the next fifteen minutes. "Ladies and gentlemen, please keep your seat belts on until seat belt sign is extinguished."

The announcement for food and refreshments was the signal Hayyan needed to spring into action. Hayyan gets up from his seat, reaches above the storage compartment, grabs his backpack, closing the storage door, then proceeds to one of the lavatories in the back of the Delta comfort section. The clanging of soda cans, coffee carafes, hot water decanters are heard as some of the flight attendants carefully maneuver their shaking and pitching catering trolleys down the aisle. The attendants begin asking passengers for their selection on food and drink as they started from their assigned sections in the cabin. Less than fifteen minutes later, Hayyan comes out of the lavatory, returning to his seat. He covertly hands out what looks like makeshift type handguns to the other three men. He gestured to the three men to get up, go to their assigned positions on the plane. Salem positions himself between rows forty-three and forty-four. Joram positions himself between rows thirty-two and thirty-three. Suske positions himself between rows seven and ten while Hayyan will force his way into the locked cockpit. On his way towards the cockpit door, Hayyan grabs senior flight attendant, Ellen Sillman, as he presses the barrel of his makeshift gun into her side. He whispers to her in a stern voice, "Do not cry out, or I will shoot you." Hayyan reaches the cockpit door, he pounds on it with his left fist while he holds the gun to Ellen Sillman's side, with his right hand demanding that the door be opened or some of the passengers will be shot at random by one of the other three men onboard the plane.

Many of the passengers in the first-class section of the cabin hear Hayyan's demented ravings as some begin to get up from their seats to survey what's going on by the cockpit door. Immediately, Suske orders the passengers to sit down and stay in their seats. One of the passengers in first class stands up demanding to know what was going on. Suske, irritated by the man's persistent squabbling, walks over, backhands him across the face. Suske, "You will stay silent! Say nothing and you will live. Complain again and I will have to silence your voice permanently," forcing the man back down in his seat.

Across from the man who was backhanded by Suske, an Army sergeant, Jason Santini on leave from Fort Drum, Jefferson NY stands up while looking at Suske saying, "All of you people are such cowards that you can only be in control of a situation by the pointing of a gun and being physically brutal to other human beings."

Suske, "Be quiet, soldier. Remember who has the gun."

Sergeant Santini, "You think you're so bad, go ahead and shoot me."

Suske, "Don't push me; I may do it."

Sergeant Santini, "Go ahead, you freakin' maggot!"

Suske raises his gun, aims and shoots the sergeant in his upper right shoulder. Some of the female passengers scream at the sound of the gun shot. Suske, "*Be quiet!* We have told you all before to be silent, say or do nothing."

Suske turns back to face Sergeant Santini as the sergeant puts steady pressure on his bleeding shoulder. Suske, "You see, soldier man, I am not afraid to shoot anyone if I'm provoked."

Sergeant Santini, "That was not too smart, idiot. If the bullet would have hit the window, at this altitude it would have depressurized the cabin and we would of went down real fast."

Suske, "You're lucky, I was aiming for your heart. Now sit down and tend to your wound, soldier."

Hayyan quickly turns around looking at Suske, then he tells Hayyan in Syrian of what had happened; Suske giving an okay sign with his left hand indicating to Hayyan that everything was under control. Hayyan turns back around demands that Ellen Sillman talk to the captain via the intercom letting him know that passengers will be killed if the cockpit door is not opened immediately. Captain answers back on the ship wide intercom, "That's impossible for any of you to have handguns. It would have been detected by the TSA X-ray scanner."

Hayyan motions to Ellen Sillman that she presses the intercom button so he can speak to the captain. Hayyan, "The handguns we smuggled onboard are made of plastic and were unassembled; TSA wouldn't have been able to tell if these parts made a gun." Hayyan continues, "The bullets were disguised in a way where they would not attract the attention of TSA if seen by the X-ray scanner."

Captain, "Allow my senior flight attendant the use of the cabin/cockpit microphone, let her tell me that you have working firearms and that the bullets are real."

Ellen Sillman presses the intercom button as she talks to the captain. "Captain, it seems as though he has some form of handgun. It's crude looking but might be effective enough to shoot a bullet out of it." Hayyan reaches into his pants pocket taking out a bullet for Ellen Sillman to describe to the captain. Ellen, "He showed me a bullet and it feels real. These people are not playing around."

Captain, "What are your demands?"

Hayyan reaches for the intercom button saying, "I want access to the cockpit. We will take control of the aircraft, deviate from the current heading. If our demands are not met, I will instruct my soldiers to choose a victim, shooting them in front of the other passengers. I believe that one of my brothers have had an altercation with one of the passengers. Luckily, the passenger was an American army soldier, but he was only slightly wounded."

Captain, "If we meet your demands, will you spare the lives of the passengers and my crew?"

Hayyan, "Meet my demands, no one will be hurt."

Captain, "Very well. I will ask my first officer to unlock the cockpit door."

Right before the cockpit door is opened, Suske, who was still positioned between rows seven and ten, comes running towards the cockpit door just as it opens. The two men rush into the cockpit. Cockpit door is locked behind them, two gunshots ring out. Passengers hearing the gun shots begin to panic. Hayyan announces from the cockpit over the cabin wide public address shouting his commands to all the passengers. Hayyan, "You will be *quiet!* You will stay in your seats, no one is to get up. If you need to relieve yourselves, one of my men will escort you. Is that clear?" Both Hayyan and Suske are at the controls, ready to make the course corrections to get to their intended destination. Hayyan, "Suske, plot a return course, set our heading for the Capitol Building in Washington. Make sure you shut off the transponder along with all acquisition lights. We can't be spotted visually or on radar."

Suske, "Understood, Hayyan. I'll make the course correction now." As the course correction is made, a red light on the T.E.O.S control panel begins to blink at one flash per second. Hayyan and Suske immediately notice the light, but do not question what it is, or what it does. They have no knowledge of the T.E.O.S system used on the aircraft. They continue flying for another ten minutes, then notice that the blinking red light is now steady, no longer flashing. Suddenly, both men hear what sounds like giant electric motors spinning up, but neither of the men have any idea of what is happening. Both engines on the Boeing B777 begin to lose power. Finally, both engines stall, stall warnings begin to sound. Plane begins losing altitude quickly, they're still over water with no land yet in sight.

Passengers begin to plea with their captures that the plane is going to crash into the ocean. Salem yells out to Joram, "What do we do? What are Hayyan and Suske doing up there? Are they in control of the plane?"

Joram, "I don't know, Salem, there must be a reason for what they're doing. Maybe something has gone wrong with the plane?"

Salem yells out to Joram, "We are going to die, we will not accomplish our jihad. May Allah forgive us."

Hayyan looks over at the comm radios knowing he cannot call for help or instructions since this would give them away that they have hijacked the passengers and crew. Suske looks over at the altimeter realizing that they're in a nosedive rapidly losing altitude as the digit counter swiftly toggles down with less than three thousand feet before they crash into the Atlantic Ocean. Suske, "Hayyan, we have failed, Allah will not be pleased."

Hayyan, "May Allah forgive us."

Crash...

Six months have passed since the crash of Delta flight *4502* bound for Dublin, Ireland, that crashed eight miles off the coast of Delaware. The aircraft had a manifest of three hundred twenty-seven passengers, a total crew compliment of thirteen including captain and first officer. The N.T.S.B. completes its final report to reveal its findings, held at an open hearing in Washington D.C. where N.T.S.B. investigative officials, general public, airline representatives, and news media along with the F.A.A. will be present.

Jackson Elliot, lead N.T.S.B. investigator, starts the open proceedings to discuss the probable causes of the Delta airlines *4502* crash. Jackson Elliot, "Good morning, ladies and gentlemen, respected airline officials, news media, members of the F.A.A. I thank you all for being here. I will now reveal all the investigation results of Delta flight *4502*. The crash occurred over the Atlantic Ocean on the evening of March 15 at around 8:03pm. As far as we can surmise, there were no survivors. The recovered data flight recorder indicated both engines at some point during the flight lost power, no attempts were made for engine re-start. Now what I am about to say has been verified thoroughly based on the recovered cockpit voice recorder. The conclusions of this N.T.S.B. panel is that the aircraft was hijacked by a terrorist group as confirmed by the FBI and CIA. At some point during the flight, terrorists forced their way into the cockpit. They made it clear to the flight crew they had handguns, shooting some of the passengers at random if the crew did not comply to their demands."

Marshall Collins, FAA senior member, "Excuse me, Mr. Elliot, I'm sorry to interrupt you, how did these terrorists manage to get guns and bullets pass the TSA check point at the airport?"

Jackson, "Mr. Collins, after talking to FBI and CIA operatives, both of them believe that this terrorist group were using handguns produced on a 3D printer. The main body of the gun would be assembled in two halves, making it harder to discern under an X-ray scan. The gun has to be assembled in order to install the metal firing pin, trigger, hammer, along the springs needed to fire the bullet. The items I mentioned before in order to make a working firearm could be concealed as parts of a ballpoint pen, a broach, a decorative knickknack; anything to throw off the TSA inspector from suspecting these parts as components for a gun. Mr. Collins, have you ever seen the movie Transformers? What they call the *autobots* start out as cars, trucks, planes, or any other mechanical piece of equipment; when needed they convert into their true form.

"Anyone creative that wants to smuggle anything pass the X-ray scanner can disguise a mechanical apparatus capable of hiding all the parts of a weapon to fool most examiners not well versed in what to look for that could build a weapon. As for the bullets, we questioned some of the TSA officers on duty that day. One officer remembers a backpack with, oddly enough, a box of crayons in it. One agent with the FBI told us that it was rumored that these terrorists could mold a small bullet (.25 caliber) then wrapped in thin lead foil incased in crayon wax. The only thing the X-ray scanner would detect, would be a box of crayons."

Marshall, "Thank you, Mr. Elliot. Please continue where you left off, so we may obtain a full transcript of what happened on that flight."

Jackson, "The captain is heard saying to the first officer, to open the cockpit door. The terrorists rushed their way into the cockpit, locking the door, seconds later, two gunshots were heard. We must assume that in order for the terrorist to gain full control of the cockpit and not run into any resistance from the flight crew, it was in their minds necessary to murder both Captain Deland, and First Officer Lopez. After the terrorists took control of the plane, one of the commands given was to change course. It was clearly heard on the voice recorder that their intended target was the Capitol Building in Washington D.C. We have been able to access the passenger manifest having been able to clear all but four passengers onboard that flight. The CIA has run an international terrorist check on the four suspected passengers. They were Syrian nationals affiliated with a Syrian terrorist group called Hayat Tahrir Al-Sham.

"Their names were Hayyan Aboud, Suske Farhi, Joram Hakim, and Salem Abdul. Both Hayyan and Suske were at the flight controls, as heard on the voice data recorder. Again, it is not certain at what point during the flight both engines stalled, causing the plane to start losing altitude. It's evident that the plane was on its return leg to the United States when it started to lose power. We examined the flight data recorder, there was no mechanical or electrical emergency reason for the T.E.O.S. system to be activated, causing both engines to stall. We have no explanation of what might have happened, we have to conclude that it might have been some form of fuel starvation anomaly."

Marshall, "Thank you, Mr. Elliot. I feel that this raises a whole new level of consciousness when terrorists are now able to bring handguns and bullets onboard a plane. They can now threaten crew members and passengers. Is there anything else you would like to add, sir?"

Jackson, "Yes, sir! On behalf of all of us at the N.T.S.B. we would like to express our deepest condolences to all those losing their dear loved ones. Especially for Captain Gregg Deland and First Officer Jerry Lopez who were brutally murdered."

Marshall, "Thank you, Mr. Elliot. Ladies and gentlemen, this concludes the N.T.S.B. public investigation report on the crash of Delta Flight *4502*. For now, the F.A.A. is satisfied with the report and will consider this case closed unless new evidence is produced shedding new light on the cause of the crash. Thank you to everyone here in attendance, have a nice day."

Chapter 7

A group of local Parisians walking down the concourse, on their way to board a flight to Norway, were proudly waving to everyone seated at the different airline gates as some of them were saying in French, *"Vive la France, mesamis"* (long live France, my friends).

It's a cool, dismal rainy afternoon, at Charles DeGaulle International Airport in Paris, with spirits high because today is (*Le Jour De La Libération*) WWII victory day that is celebrated throughout France every May 8th since 1945. An Airbus A380, Air France flight *706* is scheduled from France to Moscow with one stop over in Warsaw, Poland. Flight crew consisted of Captain Renee LeBeau and First Officer Roberta Bernard. All passengers have boarded, aircraft is towed back from the aerobridge, pilots have started both engines, are now heading for the side apron, to wait for take-off clearance. Captain, "Tower, requesting take-off clearance, Air France *706*."

Tower, "Air France *706*, proceed to runway zero-nine right, hold for clearance."

Captain, "Roger, tower, Air France *706* will hold."

While the flight crew waits for an aircraft on final approach to land, Captain LeBeau was in conversation with his first officer Roberta Bernard. Captain, "Roberta, are you going to visit any sites in Moscow while we're there?"

First Officer, "I'm not sure, sir. I've been on long shifts lately, could use the time to catch up on some much-needed sleep."

Captain, "Me, I thought I would visit Red Square and St. Basil's Cathedral, it's been awhile. That's if I don't fall asleep first."

Just then, the call from the tower comes through that Air France *706* is cleared for departure. Captain, "Roger, tower, cleared for take-off on runway zero-nine right, Air France *706*."

Tower, "Have a good flight, Air France *706*."

Captain, "Roger tower, thank you, Air France *706* is clear. Well, Roberta, just another flight to Russia."

First Officer, "Yes, sir!"

It's a 5-hour 30-minute flight including the stop-over in Warsaw Chopin Airport, Poland until reaching Domodedovo Moscow Airport, Russia. Aircraft takes off, rotates, then is instructed to climb to thirty-five thousand feet with course heading to Poland. Captain LeBeau mentioned to First Officer Bernard that it was just another flight to Russia. As events are to unfold while in flight it will soon become evident that this is not going to be just another routine flight to Russia. Two hours into the flight, three young men seated in *14J*, *14K*, and *14L,* are having a conversation in their native tongue about what is to go down on Air France flight *706*. "Do you understand what needs to happen? Take one of these sharpened pieces of plastic that you can use as a weapon should any of the passengers try to overtake or attack you. Ali and I will approach the cockpit door security lock, open it to get inside as quickly as possible. Ali, you stand by me at the cockpit door, rush in before the flight crew has a chance to block the doorway. We will also have Muhammad to act as a distraction so passengers don't get suspicious of what we are doing near the cockpit door," As Ali Sarraf is now being assigned his task.

As the terrorist co-pilot answers, "I understand, Milad."

Milad Isa, the assigned terrorist pilot, gives his instructions to the third terrorist, "Are you ready? Let's go! Kasim, watch to make sure that no passengers get suspicion of what is going on up front."

Kasim Daher answers, "Yes, Milad. I will be vigilant."

Both Milad and Ali approach the security keypad, Milad pulls out from his backpack, an electronic box that he proceeds to place directly over the keypad. Milad presses a red push button that activated the box, after a few seconds, the electromagnetic locks to the cockpit door release. Ali is already in position by the cockpit door to push the door in, then holding it for Milad to get in. Captain LeBeau and First Officer Bernard are caught off guard, but remain seated.

Milad, "Stay where you are. Keep your hands where we can see them, touch nothing!"

Captain, "What do you want?"

Milad, "We want control of the airplane. As long as you cooperate, no one will get hurt. We intend to fly to Al-Asad Air Base in Al Anbar, Iraq; hold both the passengers and crew hostage until all of our demands are met. At which time we will release everyone unharmed."

Captain, "Why are you doing this?"

Milad, "We are not part of any one terrorist group. We just want to show to the world that we need to be taken seriously, be given the respect that we deserve. The United States especially must be aware that we have rights and needs too."

Captain, "So now what?"

Milad, "We must put you to sleep. I have a light Chloroform mixture that we brought onboard, we will put you and your first officer out until we land in Al Anbar to make our demands known. You will not be killed! Allah as my witness, our intention is not to kill you."

Captain, "Why can't you just tie us up, keeping us awake."

Milad, "I'm sorry, Captain, I can't do that, these are our rules of engagement."

Captain, "Okay! Swear to me that my crew and passengers will not be harmed!"

Milad, "Captain, you have my word that no one will be harmed."

Captain, "Very well." Milad and Ali administer the chloroform mixture-laden handkerchiefs over the noses of the captain and first officer until both of them are out.

Both Milad and Ali remove the crew, placing them face down on the cockpit floor, binding their hands with plastic tie straps, then placing pieces of duct tape over their mouths. Both Milad and Ali get into the cockpit seats, buckle their seat harnesses, then begin to look over all the gauges, taking note of the plane's airspeed, altitude, fuel supply, engine status; then scan the Flight Management System, checking all waypoints programmed between France, Poland, with final destination being Moscow. Milad, "Ali, shut off the automatic pilot, get ready to make the course correction to Al Asad Air Base."

Ali, "I'll soon shut off the automatic pilot, I'm plotting the course correction now."

Milad, "I pray to Allah, that we will be triumphant."

Warsaw Chopin Airport, Air Traffic Controller Peter Kowalski, while on duty looking at his radar screen, notices that Air France *706* has inadvertently changed course straying from its original flight plan; now heading in a southeasterly direction, away from the airport. Peter immediately notifies the Air Traffic Control lead shift manager stating that Air France flight *706* is no longer on its filed IFR flight plan to Warsaw Chopin Airport. Alex Nowak approaches Peter's radar screen, also verifying that the flight is definitely off course. Peter looking up at Alex asks if he should contact flight *706* to confirm with the flight crew if they are having mechanical or electrical problems forcing the flight to veer off course. Alex, "Yes, go ahead, Peter, contact Air France *706*, ask if they are in any difficulty and do they need assistance." Peter, "Yes, sir, I'll call them now."

Peter, "Air France flight *706,* this is Warsaw Chopin tower; have noticed you are off course, is there an emergency or do you require any assistance?" Peter releases the transmit button on his microphone then waits for a reply. Peter gets no reply from the flight crew. Deciding to repeat his message again. Peter, "Air France flight *706*, this is Warsaw Chopin tower, we have noticed that you are off course, is there an emergency or do you require any assistance?"

Peter, "Alex, I've sent my message to Air France *706* twice, but no reply, what else should I try to get in touch with them?"

Alex, "Peter, let me try something." Alex sits next to Peter, then plugs in his microphone/headset into an input jack of Peter's radio set. Alex, "Air France *706*, this is Warsaw Chopin Airport, we are considering that your communication radios may be inoperative. Please follow my instructions so we can determine that, as the problem. For the next minute, please turn your transponder on then off every 10 seconds. If you are able to receive and not send, then your aircraft transponder ID will turn on and off every 10 seconds indicating that you at least can receive. We will be able to see the toggling of the transponder on the radar screen causing the ID to disappear then reappear." Alex waits the minute, then longer, hoping that the flight crew received the transmission and are preparing for the test. Over two minutes go by with no change to the status of the transponder on the radar screen.

Peter, "Alex, do you suspect that the aircraft has been hijacked by a group of terrorists and they're refusing to answer because that might give them away?"

Alex, "There is no way to tell for sure." Alex contacts the 33rd Air Base at Powidz. Talks to Commanding Officer Captain Jan Lewinski of the base clueing him into what's going on with Air France *706*. Tells him that the flight had a scheduled stopover in Poland. After the Base commander gets all the specifics from lead Air Traffic Controller Alex, he decides to dispatch a pair of F16 tactical fighters to intercept the airliner so the fighter pilots can make visual contact determining what is going on with the aircraft.

Milad, "Ali, the tower at Warsaw Chopin Airport has tried to contact us more than once asking if we are in any kind of trouble or if we need assistance. Should we answer or do we stay silent?"

Ali, "If we answer, Milad, can we fool them into believing that we are the flight crew?"

Milad, "That is a chance my friend I don't wish to explore."

Ali, "Milad, they have asked us if we are in an emergency situation or if we just need assistance. Maybe we can create a situation where they'll think that we have run into a major crisis and have lost control of the aircraft and our communication systems are down."

Milad, "It could work Ali. By the time they send search groups out to look for the plane, we will be in Al Anbar, then we can make our demands to the Iraqi and United States governments."

Ali, "Could work, my brother."

Milad, "Okay, Ali, shut off the transponder, we don't need for them to track our exact position on radar any further."

Ali, "Done; transponder is deactivated."

Retired British Army Staff Sergeant Reginald (Reggie) Upton is seated in *19C*. He notices that the aircraft changes course before its scheduled stopover in Poland, before continuing on to Moscow, instead the plane makes a turn to the southeast. He leaves his seat as he heads towards the cockpit. He is met by flight attendant Muhammad Tohan that was near the cockpit door; Reggie asked why the flight crew has changed course. Muhammad went on to explain that there is a high-altitude super cell that the pilots wanted to avoid. As soon as the plane clears the storm, they would get back to the original course. Reggie accepts the explanation given to him by flight attendant Muhammad. Reggie returns to his seat not knowing what is really happening in the cockpit. Back in the cockpit as the course correction is made, a red light on the T.E.O.S. control panel begins to blink at about one flash per second. Milad and Ali immediately notice the light, but do not question what it is or what it does. Neither one, is not familiar with the T.E.O.S. system used on the aircraft. They continue to fly for another ten minutes noticing that the blinking red light is now steady, no longer flashing. Suddenly, the two men hear what sounds like giant electric motors winding up and getting faster turning, but neither of the men has any idea of what was happening.

Next, all four engines on the airbus A380 begin to lose power. Finally, all engines stall, restart engine warnings begin to sound in the cockpit. Plane begins to lose altitude quickly; they are still nowhere near their destination. Milad does not radio for help or instructions since this would give them away that they have hijacked the passengers and crew of flight *706*. Ali looks over at the altimeter realizing that they are in a nosedive rapidly losing altitude. With less than three-thousand-two-hundred feet before they crash somewhere in the Turkish desert. Ali, "We are not going to make it, Milad."

Milad, "Obviously, our cause was never to be. Good bye, my brother, see you in heaven."

Crash...

The Air France flight was close to a half hour ahead of the dispatched Polish fighters; pilots radio in to get permission to cross Turkish airspace. They were able to get the last known position reported from Turkish Bursa Yenisehir Airport. They continue to fly in a southeasterly direction, as they reach the Turkish desert, they spot the crashed remains of the Air France A380. Both fighter pilots do a couple of low altitude fly-bys then alert Turkish authorities they have spotted the plane with survivors walking away from the wreck.

It has been five and half months since the crash of Air France *706* bound for Moscow. The B.E.A. (Bureau of Enquiry and Analysis) completes its final report revealing its findings to the public and the E.A.S.A. (European Aviation Safety Agency) in an open hearing held in Paris, France. Mrs. Emma Caron—Lead B.E.A. Investigator, "Bonjour and good morning, esteemed members of the E.A.S.A., everyone in attendance this morning. I thank you all for being here, I will now go over all the investigation results of Air France flight *706*. The crash happened four hundred kilometers (two hundred forty-nine miles) east of Ankara, Turkey. In the middle of an unpopulated desert area on the afternoon of May 8th at around 5:03pm local time. So far, we have been able to deduce that out of a passenger list of four hundred eighty-three, two hundred sixty-one died, one hundred eight were injured, seven crew members died, including the captain and first officer. The recovered flight data recorder indicated that all four engines at some point during the flight lost power; no attempt was made for engine re-start. From the recovered cockpit voice recorder, the names of two of the terrorists at the flight controls have been identified with the help of Interpol and Scotland Yards. Their names were Milad Isa and Ali Sarraf. They have been traced back to Iraq as their point of origin but have no association with any known Iraqi terrorist groups. The one factor that was discovered about them is that they possessed an advanced knowledge of electronics and computer programming. They were able to devise an electronic disruptor that would scrabble the decoder/encoder circuits in the keypad, override, then reset the electromagnetic locks to open the cockpit door. From the cockpit voice recorder, we learned that both the captain and first officer where both knocked out using chloroform that the terrorists brought onboard. We were also able to learn that the terrorist had an accomplice. It turns out to be one of the flight attendants.

"Muhammad Tohan works for Air France; was able to help the terrorists with their attempts at disrupting the keypad lock, getting into the cockpit. Tohan survived the crash, and has been interrogated by Interpol to find out more about his involvement with the terrorists. On a side note, after studying the data voice recorder, Warsaw Chopin Airport Air Traffic Controllers tried on a few occasions to contact the flight crew of Air France *706*. No reply came back, which lead the tower to surmise that there was either mechanical, electrical, or possibly radio communication problems. In an effort to determine the exact reason for the lack of communication, one of the controllers called the 33rd Air Base in Powidz where two F16s were dispatched to make visual contact to confirm on the status of the aircraft. We have also learned of a retired British Army Staff Sergeant Reginald Upton onboard the flight that spoke to Muhammad Tohan asking why the plane had changed course. Fortunately, retired Staff Sergeant Upton survived the crash as well, and has cooperated fully with the B.E.A. to extract anything that might be of interest when he spoke to Tohan. The terrorists had weapons that were passed through the security checkpoint, using very thin long plastic shims that were sharpened to razor sharpness made to resemble a type of utility cutter knife blade. Dangerous enough to kill someone if the blade was placed along the victim's neck, swiftly swiped to cut an artery. Their objective was to hold passengers and crew hostage at Al Asad Air Base in Al Anbar Iraq until U.S. and Iraqi authorities offered some sort of exchange to let the hostages free. The wreckage of the Airbus A380 was thoroughly examined. No sign of mechanical or electrical engine failure was apparent but the onboard T.E.O.S system might have been activated prematurely. We can only presume that the terrorists, not being familiar with all the aircraft controls, might have accidently switched control systems off causing all four engines to stall in flight. We are grateful that being the kind of aircraft it was, luckily not crashing into an ocean made it possible for some of the passengers and crew to survive, along with retrieving both flight and data recorders in pristine condition. In conclusion, we at the B.E.A. cannot unequivocally confirm the exact reason for the Airbus A380 crash. For now, there are still unanswered questions."

Jacques Fournier, E.A.S.A. Senior Member, "Thank you, Mrs. Caron. After hearing the details behind the crash of Air France flight *706*, we at the E.A.S.A. must conclude that there are still questions that cannot be answered as to why the aircraft basically just fell out of the sky. For now, the E.A.S.A. must accept the finding from the B.E.A. closing this investigation until further evidence is produced in conjunction with this crash. Thank you for your attendance at this public hearing. Have a peaceful day. *Au-revoir* (good bye)."

Chapter 8

Inventor Joseph Sherman is becoming gravely concerned over the fact that within a relatively short period of time, two airliners have inexplicably crashed. One into the ocean over United States waters as it made its way back to the mainland taking the lives of everyone onboard. While yet another airliner crash lands in a desert in Turkey with many dead and injured passengers. Joe needs to discover what unknown catalyst can overtake and manipulate these planes where the outcome has always been disastrous. He is quite aware from the reports he acquired from the N.T.S.B. in Washington and the Paris branch of the B.E.A that both of these flights were hijacked by terrorists. Joe starts to analyze whether the terrorists, as they fumbled their way through a plethora of countless switches and levers, inadvertently started a sequence of underlying reactions unbeknownst to them switching on the T.E.O.S. system going automatic, that generated a chain of events that lead to the eventual demise of aircraft, crew, and passengers.

Joe decides to reach out to his friend Ryan Comfort at R&R Industries. If anyone could formulate a reason for all these tragedies occurring, it would be the senior chief engineer that helped research and develop the whole system. Joe decides to call Ryan Comfort to tap into his vast technical reservoir of knowledge on what might have caused the recent plane crashes in the United States and Turkey. Joe, "Hi Ryan! How are you, how's the whole family?"

Ryan, "Doing good, how are you and your family doing?"

Joe, "Everything is fine. Ryan, I called you to see if you can figure out what's going on with all these planes that are falling out of the sky, and no one seems to know why?"

Ryan, "Joe, is there any way you could possibly come to R&R Industries?"

Joe, "Sure, Ryan, I'll pack a bag and try to be on the next plane out."

Ryan, "I would really appreciate it. What I have to tell you must be told in confidence and behind closed doors, not on the phone."

Joe arrives at the front security desk of R&R Industries. He gives the security guard his driver's license along with his special R&R Industries security clearance badge. Front desk security guard, "Thank you, Mr. Sherman. I'll call Mr. Comfort let him know you're here in the lobby."

Ten minutes pass, then one of the main lobby elevator doors open as Ryan Comfort steps out proceeding toward where Joe was seated. Joe stands extending his right hand to shake Ryan's. Ryan, "Good morning, Joe, how was your flight?"

Joe, "Smooth."

Ryan, "Joe, let's go upstairs to my office."

Ryan and Joe walk towards the main lobby elevators as the door opens on one of the elevators, with both men stepping in. Elevator reaches the second floor, both men step out as they walk towards Ryan's office.

Ryan, "Step into my office."

Joe, "Okay."

Ryan, "Let me close the door. Joe, what I am about to tell you is in the strictest of confidence, if anyone from the government ever found out, I could end up in jail on charges of conspiracy for a very long time. During the development of the individual component systems for T.E.O.S, remember those special engineers from the military and government special ops group?"

Joe, "Sure, I do!"

Ryan, "They were messing around with the programming for the activation sequence software that's used on T.E.O.S. I don't know exactly what they did, I'll bet good money that something was altered, but I just don't know."

Joe, "Damn! Those bastards. I always had a bad gut feeling that they were going to do more than just do simulations to determine the systems potential. Okay, thanks, Ryan. I have to do my own investigation into what they did to change how T.E.O.S works. I promise you, my friend, that this conversation never took place."

Ryan, "Thanks, Joe. I like to be able to be with my wife, watch my kids grow up," as Ryan places a half smile on his face.

Joe, "I'll keep in touch when I can, see you later."

Ryan, "See you! Be careful out there."

Joe, "I will, bye."

Joe arrives on an afternoon flight into Dulles International Airport. Joe confirms his rental car, then finding it, heads out at the worst time when traffic both in and out of Washington D.C. was going to be total gridlock. First stop would be the Washington headquarters for the National Transportation Safety Board (N.T.S.B.). Joe parks his rental car in the parking garage, walking over the skybridge linking the garage to the federal building for the N.T.S.B. Joe was able to setup an appointment over the phone in the hopes of meeting with the lead investigator for the *4502* crash. He is to meet with Jackson Elliot, who was the lead investigator during the crash of Delta Airlines flight *4502* bound for Dublin, Ireland. Joe is hoping to probe the N.T.S.B. to see if they know anything. He knows now from Ryan Comfort that the military, with those government operatives, might have been messing around with T.E.O.S. during the research and development stage. Joe patiently waits in the main lobby until the desk receptionist calls to Joe informing him that Mr. Elliot will see him now. An escort is dispatched to bring Joe from the lobby to Mr. Elliot's office. Both individuals reach Mr. Elliot's office as the escort walks in ahead of Joe to announce that Mr. Joseph Sherman is here to see you. The escort motions to Joe to step into the office. Joe walks up to the large heavy looking mahogany desk; he extends his right hand. Mr. Elliot gets up from his executive leather chair to greet Joe. Jackson Elliot is a medium build man in his forties with salt and pepper hair and a well-trimmed mustache to match.

Joe, "Good morning, Mr. Elliot. Thank you for seeing me today."

Jackson Elliot, "Your welcome, Mr. Sherman, please call me Jackson. How can I help you?"

Joe, "Jackson, I am really concerned with these flights that, for some reason or another, are just falling out of the sky. I refer, of course, to Delta Airlines flight *4502* bound for Dublin, and Air France *706* bound for Moscow."

Jackson, "Yes we heard about Air France *706* from our aeronautic counterparts at the B.E.A. in Paris."

Joe, "Maybe I'm just being an overprotective parent towards my invention but I don't want anyone to suspect that my system has gone rogue, turning into a killing machine."

Jackson, "Mr. Sherman, what gives you the impression that T.E.O.S. should be your one and only arbitrary reason for planes crashing?"

Joe, "It seems odd that a plane in-flight, all systems operating normally, suddenly engines lose power, they stall then plane goes down."

Jackson, "Here at the N.T.S.B. we subscript to the same conclusions. What would make a perfectly sound aircraft, for no apparent reason, just crash?"

Joe, "I sometimes, on occasion, keep thinking that maybe there might be an external force unknown to anyone that can take control of an aircraft at random."

Jackson, "That, we can't speculate on. We don't have enough evidence to prove it."

Joe, "I understand. Well, I won't take up any more of your time, Mr. Elliot. You have been very helpful in trying to shed some light on many dark and elusive questions that still linger."

Jackson, "You're welcome, Mr. Sherman. I hope that the clouds of doubt will break soon so all of us will be enlightened by what's found in regards to all these tragedies."

Joe, "Thank you for your words of encouragement. Take care, Mr. Elliot."

Jackson, "You as well, Mr. Sherman. Allow me to page an escort that will bring you to the main lobby. I'm sure you can see your way out."

Joe, "Yes, thank you." Joe was unsuccessful to extract any sort of clues that would be helpful in determining what is going on with these plane crashes. His next visit to the F.A.A. might reveal better results.

Joe makes an early morning phone call to the F.A.A. hoping he can schedule a meeting to speak to Marshall Collins, senior member of the F.A.A. Joe dials his cell phone then waits for someone to answer. He gets the phone greeting from the front desk receptionist. He then asks if it would be possible to setup a meeting with Marshall Collins. The front desk puts him on hold then after a few moments, replies that Mr. Collins is away on assignment. Joe is told that he can meet with Rachael Hart who is handling Mr. Collins duties and responsibilities while he is away. Joe agrees setting up the meeting for late morning. Joe arrives at the F.A.A. parking garage, then makes his way to the front lobby of the federal building where the F.A.A. headquarters are located. Joe reaches the front lobby desk, explains that he has a late morning appointment with Ms. Rachael Hart. Front desk receptionist dials Rachael's office telling her that Joseph Sherman was there to see her. Joe is still searching for clues that the F.A.A. might provide more comprehensive data towards the crash of Delta flight *4502* bound for Dublin, Ireland. He hopes the F.A.A. can also divulge speculative details about Air France flight *706* that crashed in the Turkish desert. As Joe waits for someone to take him to see Rachael Hart, he hears a pair of high heels clicking from down the hallway. The high heel clicking gets louder as they approach the front lobby desk. A middle aged tall slender brunette with glasses leans slightly over the counter then tells the receptionist that she will bring Mr. Sherman back to her office. Rachael turns her head as she focuses on where Joe is sitting. She walks over asking, "Mr. Sherman?"

Joe gets up from his seat, as he replies, "Yes, I'm Joseph Sherman."

Rachael, "Good morning, Mr. Sherman," shaking his hand then asking him to follow her down the hall to her office. They reach her office; she asks Joe to step into her office as she closes the door behind her.

Rachael, "We have been expecting you."

Joe, "Boy! News does travels fast in Washington, doesn't it?"

Rachael, "We want to get to the bottom of the this as much as you do, Mr. Sherman. We know that you have serious concerns about the T.E.O.S. system."

Joe, "Okay, Rachael; if I may call you, Rachael?"

Rachael, "That's fine, Mr. Sherman. Should I call you Joseph or Joe?"

Joe, "Joe will be fine. Okay, Rachael, so what does the F.A.A. know, that the rest of us don't?"

Rachael, "What I'm about to say cannot be confirmed nor denied by anyone here at the F.A.A. One of our crash analysts did flight performance simulations on the Delta flight *4502* and Air France flight *706*. Based on data extracted from both flight recorders, our crash analyst believes that whenever the aircraft made a course change, is when the sequence of events began to happen. Not much after, the engines stalled and the plane crashed."

Joe, "That's very interesting. Do you believe that there's an outside entity responsible for this to happen?"

Rachael, "None of us here at the F.A.A. can be certain of anything. As for the analysis done by our crash expert, we support this theory very strongly at the F.A.A. but yet it is not open for discussion at any level until more conclusive proof can be obtained."

Joe, "I'm going to perform my own flight simulations to see if I get similar results. If the results match, then we may have something to go on. I'm fortunate that since I have worked with many top engineers and designers at R&R Industries, I may be able to persuade them to indulge me in performing a variety of simulations using mechanical and electrical faults introduced into the simulation, then watching how each of the parameters effect the performance of the engines until we get the exact chain of events leading up to an engine stall. Let me get going, thank you for your time and valuable information you have shared with me today."

Rachael, "You're welcome, Mr. Sherman. If we can be of further assistances, please let us know."

Joe, "Will do. Good bye."

Now there is only one last visit while in Washington D.C.; the U.S. Department of Homeland Security. Joe is hoping that whomever he talks to will give him additional clues as to what is going on with these air disasters.

Joe's goal is to see if either Homeland Security or even the Transportation Security Administration (T.S.A.) can provide more details then what the N.T.S.B. or F.A.A. were able to.

Before Joe left the F.A.A. federal building, he asked the front lobby receptionist whether she could provide him with the main phone number to Homeland Security. The receptionist found the number writing it down and handing it to Joe. When Joe got to his parked car, he called the number for Homeland Security as he introduced himself then stating the purpose for his call asking if he could setup an appointment at the last minute to talk to a representative while he was still in Washington D.C. After waiting a few minutes on the phone, an answer came back that he would be able to meet with someone on such short notice. Grateful, Joe thanks the person on the other end of the phone then proceeds to the Homeland Security building. Joe arrives, parks then heads for the front lobby desk. He identifies himself, then tells them he setup a last-minute appointment to meet with a Homeland Security representative. After a few moments on the phone, the front lobby receptionist places the phone back on the hook telling Joe that someone will come to greet him taking him to a waiting representative. As Joe waits in the lobby, he is looking over some of his notes that he jotted down while speaking to both N.T.S.B. and F.A.A. officials. As he turns a page in his notebook, a young man approaches asking, "Mr. Sherman?"

Joe looking up replies, "Yes!"

"My name is Tim Hodges, I'm here to take you to see Mrs. Fitzgerald. You'll be meeting with her."

Joe, "Great," Joe closes his notebook, putting in his briefcase as he stands then follows Tim to Mrs. Fitzgerald's office.

Tim stops at the office saying to Joe, "Here you are, Mr. Sherman."

Joe, "Thank you, Tim, have a nice day."

Tim, "You as well, sir."

Joe walks into the office. Joe meets with Xavier Fitzgerald, head of the T.S.A. department in the Washington D.C. office.

Joe, "Good morning, Mrs. Fitzgerald. Thank you for seeing me under such short notice."

Xavier, "Your welcome, Mr. Sherman."

Joe, "I wish that the circumstances were of a happier nature. I'm here today to discuss with you any details that might prove helpful in determining what when wrong with the Delta Airlines and Air France flights that crashed. As I have already expressed to both the N.T.S.B. and the F.A.A., there has to be a perfectly rational explanation to the accidents that have occurred in recent years."

Xavier, "Is there anything particular you wish to discuss or share with us, Mr. Sherman?"

Joe, "I'm still looking for answers myself. I was hoping that T.S.A had some kind of evidence that would prove why these planes have crashed. Have any of your officers at any of the airports around the country seen or reported anything of suspicion coming through the X-ray scanners? As an example, how about something like an electronic jamming device of sorts that could disrupt the T.E.O.S system? To partially or prematurely activate, then close off the engine intakes causing engines to stall?"

Xavier, "No, sir! If any of our people would have seen something that suspicious, it would have immediately been confiscated, then sent to the Washington labs for analysis."

Joe, "Sorry, I didn't mean to belittle your agency or its employees in saying that anything out of line would simply be allowed through and never be questioned."

Xavier, "I understand your frustration, Mr. Sherman. I realize that you are just trying to vindicate your invention since so many near-tragic accidents have been avoided thanks to T.E.O.S."

Joe, "I will admit that this is going to be a hard nut to crack. In about a week, I'm heading back to R&R Industries to study all the test data and flight performances that were done on T.E.O.S. Maybe it was just missed, there is some type of glitch or anomaly that was overlooked, and was thought to be normal for the system when it was activated."

Xavier, "Well, sir! I wish you and the team at R&R Industries the best of luck and good hunting. Hope you find something that you can then share with the rest of the world."

Joe, "If we find it, the whole world will know. Then it will be back to the drawing board to fix the problem."

Xavier, "Is there anything else that the T.S.A can help you with today, Mr. Sherman?"

Joe, "No, you have been an inspiration to me because by talking about this, bouncing ideas off of you, it has opened my mind up to the possibilities that the system may not be infallible. Thank you for your time and cooperation on this. I promise you that anything we find; the proper authorities will be made aware of."

Xavier, "Thank you, Mr. Sherman. That's appreciated. Have a great rest of the day,"

Joe, "I'll be flying back home today."

Xavier, "Have a safe flight."

Joe, "Thank you." Joe prepares to head back home on an evening flight. After he's home for a couple days, he plans on going to R&R Industries to look over all the test and performance data acquired during the different early stages of research and development on T.E.O.S.

Chapter 9

After Joe packs his carryon luggage and backpack, he decides to give his wife Tracy a call since there was still plenty of time until Joe had to go make his flight home. "Good evening, honey. How are you doing?"

Tracy, "I'm doing fine, babe. How was Washington?"

Joe, "Ack! It's Washington; same crap, different day."

Tracy, "I'm sorry you had a lousy stay while you were there."

Joe, "I'm just very disappointed, honey, that after talking to officials at the N.T.S.B., F.A.A., and Homeland Security, I have to come back home with no more insight then when I first arrived."

Tracy, "You're not going to give up, are you?"

Joe, "No way. This is very important to me. I must know what's going on to determine if what has happened with those two airliners was just freak accidents or should there be a real concern with T.E.O.S."

With all that has been going on, Joe is anxious to get home to his wife and kids, spend a couple of quality days with the family before he heads back to R&R Industries. Joe, "Honey, let me go. I have to checkout, wait for a cab,

106

hopefully, I can get one with enough time to spare, get to the airport, then make my flight."

Tracy, "Ok, Joe, have a safe flight, see you soon. I love you!"

Joe, "Love you too, bye." Joe stuffs his cell phone in his pants' left pocket, grabs his carryon and backpack, shuts the light off in the room, closing the door, as he exits into the hallway. Joe takes the elevator, gets off on the ground floor, walking over to the front service desk. He turns in his key card, gets a receipt, walks through the automatic sliding front doors of the hotel, then stands along with a group of people waiting for valets or cabs. As he eagerly waits for a cab outside the hotel, in the meantime, makes idle conversation with some of the other guest while he waits. A cab finally shows up, which Joe immediately flags down. The driver steps out from the cab, opens the trunk as he takes Joe's luggage placing it in the trunk then slamming the trunk lid. Joe gets in the cab settling in for the ride to the airport.

Ajit Ramon, "Good evening, sir, where may I take you?" the cab driver had a definite accent as he spoke to Joe.

Joe, "Dulles."

Ajit, "Good airport; easy to get in and out. What airline are you flying?"

Joe, "South Best Way Airlines."

Ajit, "Oh! Another great choice, sir."

Joe looks over to get the driver's name from his ID badge. "How are you, Ajit?"

Ajit, "I am very well, thank you."

Joe, "Ajit, was that cab driver's strike here in Washington ever settled?"

Ajit, "Partially, sir! The dispatchers want a bigger cut from all the fares. We are not done with the negotiations."

Joe, "Well, for the sake of all the cab drivers in town, I hope all of you do well with the settlement."

Ajit, "Thank you, for your concern. Sir, I do not want to alarm you but I have noticed that a black SUV has been following us for some distance now."

Joe, "Don't be too concerned about it. Maybe it's someone trying to find their way to the airport, they thought following you might get them there."

Ajit answers sounding a bit apprehensive, "Maybe, sir."

Joe's cab continues on to the airport when out of a side street, another black SUV turns onto the roadway getting in front of Joe's cab. The black SUV begins to quickly pump the brakes, slowing down, forcing Ajit to press hard on his brakes to avoid hitting the back of the vehicle. Ajit tries to swing around the SUV, but it counters Ajit's move. The SUV slows down even more; again, Ajit tries to swing around the SUV but again it swings directly in front of Ajit's cab. Ajit, "I don't understand why someone is doing this?"

Joe, "I don't know either, but getting into an accident won't solve anything. Be careful; let's see how this plays out."

The SUV in front of the cab makes a quick stop forcing Ajit to cut the wheel sharply to the right in order to avoid hitting the SUV. Passenger door of the SUV opens, a dark silhouetted figure emerges, walking towards the cab. He takes hold of the passenger side door handle, opening the door. He sits in the front seat of the cab, tells the cab driver to follow the SUV in front of him. The uninvited passenger turns his body halfway to face Joe, telling him, "Mr. Sherman, you will meet with someone that will explain everything that has been going on."

Joe acknowledges with a nod, says nothing.

The cab along with the front and rear SUV escorts arrive at an old abandon underground train tunnel. Joe is asked by the uninvited passenger to step out of the cab, then follow. The uninvited passenger turns to Ajit telling him to stay in the car, not to leave. He continues, "When we are done talking to your fare, he'll be returned, you can then take him to the airport."

Ajit, "Okay."

Joe enters the tunnel opening as he walks down a long dark corridor. At the end of corridor, a large main concourse is revealed where Joe is directed by the SUV figure to sit at a table with chair that has been provided. Joe looks around; but can't make out much of what he surveys due to the very low lighting where he's sitting. He hears footsteps, noticing figures emerging from around a corner as he makes sure that he'll get a number on how many of these figures he counts. The figures approach a larger table with chairs about fifteen feet away from him. Then he realizes, *If I get a count, what the heck am I going to do with that number? Stupid! that was a dumb idea.* When the last individual is seated, Joe counts eight people at the table for the heck of it. Then a set of flood lamps are turned on so Joe's face can be seen but he can't make out those seated away from him. Joe tries to squint as he tries to adjust his eyes to the bright lamps. One solitary figure walks to the chair located centrally to the table where the others are seated. Then says, "Good evening Mr. Sherman."

Joe, "Good evening. Who are you people?"

Centralized figure, "In the interest of secrecy and plausible deniability, I am to be addressed only as Mr. R., I apologize for the cloak and dagger, but it is necessary."

Joe, "Why have you brought me here?"

Mr. R., "You are here, Mr. Sherman, because you have been asking many questions while in Washington. This could eventually lead to misinformation leaking out that could severely compromise the effectiveness and true function of T.E.O.S."

Joe, "What does T.E.O.S have to do with all this?"

Mr. R., "We have found the perfect vehicle to use as a method of destroying any would-be terrorists trying to hijack a plane to satisfy their sadistic whims. Hijackers then crash into skyscrapers; vital government buildings where innocent lives are lost because of mad suicidal religious fanatics."

Joe, "That is all well and good, but how does the government feel about purposely killing innocent people aboard those planes?"

Mr. R., "Mr. Sherman, I'm sure you remember September 11, 2001 very well, correct? The world on that day suffered a lost that can never be measured or reclaimed by retribution nor forgiveness. We are the covert guardians of this country. We believe that there can be no greater place on this planet to live, to be free, then the United States of America. Some of us accept the inevitable sacrifices of some for the good of all. If this means that some must die, it's a calculated gamble that must be taken in order to ensure that no terrorists ever conceive the notion of hijacking a plane without the terrible repercussions they themselves will be levied too. To do what they want, glorifying themselves, so even in death they can still be blessed by Allah, then given the rights to heaven."

Joe, "Okay. So how do you stall the engines on a plane?"

Mr. R., "Alright, Mr. Sherman. I'm going to tell you how it's done. If I don't tell you now, you will just find other ways to get the answers you're looking for. You are the inventor; you deserve as much. I will tell you that your system has not turned rogue, it is now under a different set of control rules. Back in the early development stages of T.E.O.S, we sent a group of military computer specialist along with our own government operatives to R&R Industries. Their task was to make essential modifications to the programming for how the system would work given particular circumstances. You know that, under normal conditions, if the jet engines are to be compromised in anyway, your system automatically begins a sequence of operations. Thus, protecting the engines from ingesting anything from birds to volcanic ash. There is additional sophisticated programming added into the command sequence for the microcomputers. Whenever the original course heading of a plane is altered from the onboard Flight Management System, this activates a secondary set of command instructions. A silent GPS signal is transmitted the moment course change is initiated. When I say silent, I mean that no audible indicators used to alert the flight crew or the terrorists of what is going on. As soon as a course correction is made, that differs from the original heading, a red light located on the T.E.O.S. control panel will begin to blink. If heading is not set back to the original course, the same red blinking light will turn solid, then the sequence for take-down will begin to stall the engines, crashing the aircraft. Terrorists will hear what sounds like giant electric motors turning. What they hear is the closing of what you call the shielding blade assembly, sealing off the intake on all engines. At that point, the engines will stall, the plane will begin to lose altitude. Even if the terrorists try to do an engine restart, the intakes are still sealed, no air will be available for the engines, in order to re-ignite the combustion chambers. Then from there, Mr. Sherman, gravity takes over, the terrorists have been stopped!"

Joe, "Wait! course corrections are made due to severe weather cells pilots are trying to avoid. Mechanical or electrical failure that forces the aircraft to have to make an emergency landing."

Mr. R., "There is more to the take-down system activation then just making a course change. The T.E.O.S system is supplied with complete aircraft operational flight data. A determination can be made on whether the course change is intentional, or due to a real time aircraft-based emergency."

Joe, "Do flight crews know about all this?"

Mr. R., "No, sir! Word of this ever leaked out, the terrorists ever found out, *game over!* It is not a perfect solution to a terrorist problem, but it is better than having the military send up a pair of F-22 Raptors to shoot an airliner down. When that happens, the government must explain to the American people, to the world, why they sent two tactical jet fighters to shoot an innocent airliner out of the sky. The aftermath of inquiries, and the barrage of political finger pointing, negative media coverage would last for months; in the end, someone would still have to be blamed. The other way, it can be blamed on mechanical, electrical, or failure from both. When the time came, we can give the people of the world our interpretation of what happened."

Some of the individuals sitting at the table, try to get Mr. R.'s. attention while he is still speaking. He finally looks over, leaning to his right as he's in a whisper with the others at the table. Mr. R., "I have been asked by my colleagues that we must have a brief interlude to discuss certain aspects of why you are here with us."

The objective by the covert group is to ensure that Joe totally understands that the success of the T.E.O.S directives must be carried out, with secrecy and denial being the only prerogatives. Mr. R., "Mr. Sherman, we realize that all this must be very stressful on you. Believe it or not, we are not monsters, nor are we inhuman. While my associates and I confer, please relax, take a moment to absorb in all that has been divulged up to this point. You are here as our guest. We will not hold you against your will. If you wish to leave, you may do so but in doing so we will not be able to finish our conversation with you. Remember, Mr. Sherman, you are not the enemy," Mr. R. "I have totally forgotten my manners. If you require something, someone will come to see you shortly to attend to anything you need."

In the interim, an attendant comes over to Joe asking if he requires a refreshment or the use of the restrooms. Joe,

"I need to use the restroom, could use a cold bottle of water."

The attendant acknowledges Joe's request; asked that he follow him, directing Joe to the restroom. He added that the bottle of water would be on the table by the time Joe got back. Ten minutes later, both Joe and those sitting away from him reconvene at their tables.

Mr. R., "Mr. Sherman, we trust that you will keep this information on the strictest level of confidentially, away from anyone that does not need to know, especially the news media. If this information was to leak out, the airline and aerospace industries in general could very well go into collapse. We must also remind you that we can't ensure the complete safety of you or your family from those that have made it their prime objective to continue upholding and enforcing this scenario. In closing, this meeting did not take place. All knowledge of this will be disavowed. We can only hope and pray that someday this system will be used only to save lives as you so passionately intended it to do. Before I have you brought back to your cab, is there anything you would like to know or add to our encounter here tonight?"

Joe, "Yes, after you took the time to outline how mine system is programmed to take down airplanes hijacked by terrorist, is there no other way to stop them without destroying the plane, flight crew, and all the passengers that unknowingly are being sentenced to their deaths? Simply because the United States, along with the rest of the countries of the world, will not make themselves accountable for their own shortcomings; yet none will take a moment out of their singular lives to figure out a creative way to stop terrorist without committing mass murder in the name of self-righteous justice."

Mr. R., "I must say Mr. Sherman you do know how to express yourself very well. Believe it or not, some of us do have families, wives, children, parents, brothers, sisters, grandparents. The only difference is that we have been charged with protecting this great country of ours. We will do whatever it takes to protect her and keep all those that need to be protected under our wing. It is not a perfect solution, but it's the only one we have for now. I hope you can accept that, Mr. Sherman."

Joe, "I have no other choice but to accept the consequence of the established actions."

Mr. R., "Thank you, Mr. Sherman. Your cab is waiting to drive you to the airport. We thank you for your contribution to a system that unfortunately must be used as a deterrent against terrorists. May you have a very safe flight."

Joe, "Thank you for allowing me into your inner circle, taking me into your confidence."

Mr. R., "Our pleasure."

Joe is asked to stay seated until all those sitting across from him walk out. The lights shining on Joe, are turned off, Joe gets up, then the escort that brought him in, motions to follow him out of the abandon train tunnel to head back to the cab where Ajit has been patiently waiting. Joe opens the passenger rear door then slips into the cab.

Ajit, "Hello, are you alright?"

Joe, "Yes, I'm fine. Go ahead Ajit, take me to the airport."

Ajit arrives at Dulles International Airport, as he prepares to drop Joe off with his luggage at South Best Way Airlines. Ajit, "Well, sir, it has been a very interesting night for me. Normally, my nights are just routine, with not much excitement."

Joe, "I'm sorry that you had to be part of that. If I would have known that I would have kept the rental car driving to the airport myself."

Ajit, "*No, no!* Do not apologize. I felt like I was in some kind of spy movie; you were James Bond or someone like that. It was scary, but exciting at the same time."

Joe, "Oh, my friend! If you only knew how close you have come to outlining the truth. Let me get out of here, I hope I didn't miss my plane?" Joe hands Ajit a fifty-dollar bill.

Ajit, "Sir! I can't break something this big."

Joe, "Keep the change, my friend. You have earned it."

Ajit, "Thank you very much. I hope to see you again someday."

Joe, "You never know how destiny can bring people together. Good bye my friend, take care of yourself."

Ajit, "Thank you, sir. You take good care of yourself as well."

Joe walks away from the cab with his luggage in tow, opens the door to the ticket lobby at South Best Way Airlines. Ajit quickly lowers the front passenger window yelling out, "Sir! I don't know your name."

Joe turns quickly to answer, "It's Joe!"

Ajit waves as he drives off.

Chapter 10

Joe arrives at the airport, as he stands around on the first floor by the luggage carousel for his carryon and backpack, he decides to call Ryan Comfort at R&R Industries.

Ryan, "R&R Industries, this is Ryan."

Joe, "Hi, Ryan, hey buddy, I'm at the airport. I'm waiting for my luggage; after I pick up the rental car, I'll head straight to R&R Industries. You want me to bring a dozen donuts? I know of a *Dunkin Donuts* that always stocks donuts you have to lick your fingers when you're done eating them."

Ryan, "Yeah, that sound great. Make sure you get some jelly-filled for me."

Joe, "You and me both. See you in a half hour."

After Joe stops to pick up some donuts, he arrives at R&R Industries. Joe walks towards the front security desk, giving the front desk guard his driver's license and R&R Industries security badge. Desk guard looks at the box of donuts in Joe's right hand. Joe notices the guard eyeing the box, as Joe warns, "Don't even think about it. You'll have a mob of engineers and designers demanding for your head."

Security guard, "I don't want that." The desk guard calls Ryan informing him that Joe Sherman is in the lobby. Ryan walks out of his office, reaches the elevators, then steps inside riding it down to the first floor. Ryan steps out of the main lobby elevator walking to the front security desk. He meets Joe at the front desk. Ryan escorts Joe upstairs, bringing him to his office. While in the elevator, without disclosing excessive details, Joe begins to explain to Ryan how the government has changed the original programming to T.E.O.S. Joe momentarily stops himself to ask a crucial question he needs an answer to.

Joe, "Ryan! Will it be safe to talk in your office? If any of this, that I'm going to tell you leaks out to these people in the government, they made it very clear that they cannot guarantee my safety or that of my family."

Ryan, "Joe, this office has been checked out by a high-end electronic bug detection scanner that Cody Banks designed, so it is impossible for this office to be bugged or have any kind of planted listening device without it being detected by Cody's scanner."

Joe, "I was told by the one covert government operative I spoke with, who only identified himself by Mr. R., that T.E.O.S. was altered from its original programming, implementing additional command instructions."

Ryan, "Wait! Wait a minute; what do you mean that you spoke to this one covert government operative?"

Joe, "Yeah, on the night I was leaving Washington to go back home, the cab I was in got intercepted by government agents with black SUV's forcing the cab driver to stop. We were led to an old, abandoned train tunnel, where I was asked to get out of the cab as the driver waited, then as I was escorted into an old abandon train tunnel. I was led into a large open area, told to sit down at a table and chair that was provided for me."

Ryan, "Jeez, Joe, weren't you scared?"

Joe, "Sure, I was, I didn't know whether they were going to just talk to me or do a New Jersey style bottom of the river tour. I was given a full disclosure to how the system was altered, they didn't spare no details.

"You know those guys that were here at R&R Industries that one week? They were responsible for making the changes, that's why they didn't want anybody going into the development lab."

Ryan, "So did this Mr. R. explain how it's done?"

Joe, "Oh yeah! T.E.O.S. becomes aware whenever there is a course correction that overrides the original course heading. When the new course change is entered, a silent signal is sent out via GPS that alerts the ground listening stations around the world, sending back a confirmation code that sets up T.E.O.S. for protect mode.

"Here is what makes the system confirm whether it is intentional or due to a real time aircraft emergency. T.E.O.S. has been tied into all aircraft operational flight data so it can detect if there is a real emergency that forces the flight crew to change course to land immediately. T.E.O.S. gets fed flight data such as engine performance, low fuel, electrical or mechanical failure, etc. But it's not only limited to the aircraft. Situations in the cabin such as a very sick passenger, heart attack victim, or just somebody drunk or disorderly that needs to be removed from the aircraft as quickly as possible."

Ryan, "How does T.E.O.S. deal with passenger issues since it is not aircraft operational related flight data?"

Joe, "I'm going to take a very large stab in the dark on this one. Since the United States government does not want to down a plane because of a sick passenger or a drunk and unruly individual, here is what I believe they might have come up with. Just before the flight crew makes a course change, they contact air traffic control, alerting them of the situation onboard the aircraft. When course change is made, a snippet of the voice transmission between flight crew and Air Traffic Control is sent as part of the telemetry data stream sent by T.E.O.S. Worldwide ground listening stations can then evaluate the onboard emergency, making the override call to cancel the take-down signal."

Ryan, "Wow! Joe, if that was true, it would be fantastic. Have a protective flight system that transmits data, then is analyzed by computer or human, then a decision is correctly made whether it is terrorism or a real flight emergency."

Joe, "That's all well and good but the part that still bothers me is that if it's a terrorists hijacking, the aircraft is rendered useless because once the engines are shut down, there is not a pray in the world."

Ryan, "Do you think there is anything that can be done to change this? I would like to think so."

Joe, "I was thinking, Ryan, would it be possible to alter the programming done to T.E.O.S., having it to where the engine intakes still closes. Have the air injection unit kick on, delivering just enough air to keep the engines alive. That could make the difference between a plane full of passengers crashing or those that have been given a chance to live."

Ryan, "Joe, I think I have the man that can make that happen and no one, especially the government, would ever know."

Joe, "Alright, Ryan, don't keep me in suspense! Who is it?"

Ryan, "It's our own Cody Banks. He's our senior electronics and computer engineer, if anyone can alter the current programming to T.E.O.S, it would be him."

Joe, "Ah! that's *great!* Do you think we can get him to collaborate with us to change the T.E.O.S. programming? Can he be trusted?"

Ryan, "Yes! I've known Cody to be many things, but a murderer, or a traitor towards a righteous cause? I don't think so. I'm sure he would like to change things around to where passengers don't die needlessly."

Joe, "Ryan, go ahead and setup a meeting with Cody. We need to talk."

Ryan, "Okay, Joe, I'll set it up."

Joe, along with Ryan in his office, waits until Cody shows up to discuss a game plan to change T.E.O.S. around. Cody finally shows up, sits down in Ryan's office after closing the office door behind him. Ryan, "Joe, I wanted to bring you up to speed that Cody has already been briefed on how T.E.O.S. has been altered when dealing with a terrorists hijacking."

Joe, "Cody, do you think you can get a good grasp of how these government guys changed T.E.O.S. around?"

Cody, "Yeah! I already managed to hack into the protected files they left behind, I was able to look at the code sets for T.E.O.S."

Ryan, "Cody can you alter the files without these guys knowing that you messed around with their programs?"

Cody, "Sure! piece of cake. Since I was able to break into their encryption algorithm, I can do it again, I'll make sure to re-encrypt the modified files into the same source folder then backdating the files to their original date."

Joe, "Cody, will it be possible to make the air injection unit supply just enough air to the engines to keep them from stalling?"

Cody, "Sure, Joe, it's a percentage ratio based on 100 percent of full power. I can adjust the amount to where the plane cannot obtain full cruising speed or a high altitude, but will maintain a safe flight level without the engines stalling."

Joe, "Perfect! after you alter the programming how do you overwrite to get the altered instruction codes to all the ground listening stations around the world?"

Cody, "We'll just use the internet to upload the codes. There is a station uplink list that has every single ground listening station from around the world. During the program upload, the primary command instruction sequence starts sending out the altered code files to every station on the list. Think of it as a bulk email message addressed to thousands of people, instead it will be uploaded to hundreds of stations."

Ryan, "Will all the stations get the new upload files?"

Cody, "Unless someone left stations out, they should all be there."

Joe, "Can anyone detect that new software is being uploaded at all these stations?"

Cody, "No, the beauty of it, is that there's a routine maintenance program that periodically goes in to check to see that everything is still functioning with no software glitches. Station operators will not see lines of code appearing on their computer screens. When the program is done, everything goes back to normal. No one is the wiser."

Joe, "Nice! how long does it take to upload the new software?"

Cody, "As long as the internet is running at full bandwidth, there should be no more of a delay then usual unless the internet is busy for some reason."

Ryan, "When can you get started on this, Cody?"

Cody, "I can start on it right away, it should only take me a couple days to test and get any bugs out of the programming. After that, you just say the word and I'll go ahead and upload it."

Ryan, "Thank you, Cody."

Joe, "Yes, Thank you, Cody."

Cody gets up from the chair heads back to the development lab to get started on rewriting the T.E.O.S. code. In the meantime, Joe and Ryan discuss the possibilities of any repercussions coming from the government if they ever found out how the T.E.O.S programming was altered. Morning at R&R Industries as Cody Banks fumbles for his keys to open up the computer development lab. Cody Banks, a mild mannered, good natured soul in his mid-thirties, that would do anything for anyone; short, well rounded with a slight receding hair line, yet possessing a knowledge in electronics and computer architecture that could rival the best of them at MIT. Making sure not to spill the full cup of hot coffee in his right hand along with his lunch bag draped across his left shoulder, as he tries to precariously juggle the coffee cup to his left hand so he can reach into his right pants pocket for the keys. He manages to open the door to the lab without suffering any burnt fingers from the hot coffee spilling over. Cody goes over to his computer station, sits down, logging in and bringing up the R&R Industries network. He maneuvers his way to the windows explorer, going into the main network drive where T.E.O.S. files are located. He expands all the files under the main directory until he finds files altered by the military engineers and government operatives that were at R&R for better than a week several years back. As Cody tries to open a file named T.E.O.S., altered programming, a dialog box appears asking for a password. Cody keeps the program file open, then from a separate window, he opens up a code encryption program he wrote many years ago using it to break encrypted passwords. Cody keeps both windows open so his program can go out looking for the password dialog. After ten minutes, of number crunching, Cody's program comes back with the password required to open the encrypted file. Cody inputs the hacked password then begins to look at the *C++* programming code as he reads instruction lines one at a time. He finally reaches the lines of code that instructs T.E.O.S. if a course change from the original coordinates has been inputted into the Flight Management System. Once identified, microcontroller circuits switch on a red warning light from the control panel, sends a silent GPS signal then waits for the confirmation override sequence that begins closing all engine intakes. Cody continues to scan the program, line by line, reading the decision part of the code looking for *<if>* and *<if not>* statements, where the program will read flight data recorder, voice data recorder, log of radio communication between flight crew and Air Traffic Control, then make a decision based on whether the course change performed by the flight crew is based on mechanical, electrical, fuel emergencies, or passenger issues such as drunk, sick, heart attack that validates the need for the flight crew to change course immediately.

Cody decides to analyze the operative-altered program in action through a simulator written to run T.E.O.S. to see how all the tampered parameters work. Cody inputs the original program as it was rewritten by military and government operatives to see how it would perform when a course change is purposely introduced into the T.E.O.S. programming. Cody initiates the simulation program, inputs into the Flight Management System, a course correction of exactly forty-five degrees from a true easterly heading. Cody waits for any change in the T.E.O.S. graphic control panel on screen. In the meanwhile, Cody sips on his coffee which has now become lukewarm, reaches for his lunch bag grabbing a cinnamon roll his wife packed for him. As he takes a bite of breakfast, a red LED indicator on the screen begins to blink at about one flash per second. Cody, looking at his aviator watch, pressed the elapsed time button to record how long the light will continue to flash at its present rate. He watches the simulation, then at about the ten-minute mark, the light turns to steady state as it no longer blinks. He notices on the screen that a warning dialog has popped up on the screen indicating that the shielding blade assemblies across all engines will begin to close. After the engine intakes are sealed off, a marquee in big, red letters scrolls across the screen, warning all engines will start to lose power, aircraft will begin to quickly descend as a graphic altimeter begins counting down. Cody stops the simulation as he decides to run his new revised programming. He repeats all the same parameters as in the operative based program, he changes the course heading, as before the red LED light begins to blink. Ten minutes after the light goes from blinking to steady state. A warning flashes on screen that engine intakes will be closing. Before intakes are closed, an indicator on a graphic panel shows the air intake doors opening, another indicator shows air injection unit starting up, maintaining only forty percent air intake volume, shielding blade assemblies begin closing off the engine intakes. Cody, once again, stops the simulation. This time, he will input all the necessary parameters to simulate a passenger that has had a heart attack needing immediate medical attention. After all the variables have been established, Cody starts the simulation to see how the T.E.O.S. system reacts when a new course change is introduced. As the simulation is running, Cody changes the course heading on the FMS from north to a westward vector. He watches to see if the system generates an alert indicating a takedown initiative. After better than ten minutes from changing course, no blinking light was evident. Cody continues watching the screen, no further changes in the simulation were observed, proving that unless the course change is intentional, the system will not become self-aware then activate. Cody calls Ryan, telling him of his success; to change how T.E.O.S. now reacts to different scenarios.

Cody walks into Ryan's office; is met by Joe who is also there waiting. Cody looks very optimistic that the new program changes will be what Joe is looking for to prevent future airline disasters. Joe, "Good morning, Cody. How are you? Well, you look really stoked up. I will assume the programming changes when well?"

Cody, "Good morning, guys, I'm doing good. I'm excited about the changes I made. The programming, all good!"

Joe, "Hey, the other day I forgot to ask you while we were talking. Did you test the altered program to make sure that T.E.O.S will still function as it should under normal circumstances?"

Cody, "Yeah! Nothing has changed there. For normal operations, better than expected."

Ryan, "Did you run into anything you weren't expecting?"

Cody, "No, I have to admit that these government guys do the old way of writing code. They make it easy to read every line because they put in a lot of comment lines that help understand their code."

Cody, feeling resentful about testing the new software, "*Damn!* I wish I had a way of testing the new instruction codes on a real aircraft. The closest I have come to testing the new programming is running it through the flight simulator developed to test T.E.O.S. I wanted to make sure that the system will always react the same if the scenario is that of a plane being hijacked. I'm pretty confident that for normal T.E.O.S. functions should all be as it is."

Ryan, "Well, Cody, you know that altering the T.E.O.S. programming on a working aircraft is a 'no cando.'

"Jeez! If upper management every found out what we have done here, they would have us put in federal prison, then throw away the key."

Joe, "And as for me, guys, I would probably get killed while serving time in prison by some undercover government operative claiming that I was selling top secret documents from jail."

Ryan, "Okay, Cody, go and start replacing the old instruction codes online with the new codes? Go work your magic."

Cody, "Yeah, I feel good about the changes. I'll go ahead and start swapping out the programs."

Cody leaves Ryan's office heading back to the development lab to begin swapping the T.E.O.S. programs.

Chapter 11

Attention please, United Airlines flight 1109 bound for Lisbon now boarding at gate 16. Passengers should have their boarding passes and passports ready, thank you.

A crisp, cool morning in San Diego, as vacationing group of seniors get ready to enjoy a well desired vacation with most of them being retirees looking forward to travel and relaxation. Along with the vacationing seniors, a group of young enthusiasts, mostly in their mid-twenties, wanting to experience the magic of the sixty's era. Some of them were overheard talking about going into some of the shops in the Soho district in Westminster to see about getting some neat, psychedelic patterned tie-dye shirts, skirts, outfits made famous during the time of the Beatles and many other groups that were part of the British invasion. The announcement is heard over the public address system of British Airways gate, informing passengers flight *235* bound for London will begin to board within a few moments. One of the gate agents at the British Airways gate desk picks up the microphone as she starts to have passengers come forward towards the gate desk. Passengers from group 1 are called so they can begin boarding. After all group 1 are boarded, the desk agent calls for all passengers from group 5, then has all passenger from group 4 board as well. Next, all passengers for group 2, followed by group 3 are the last groups to be called to board. As the last of the passengers place their carryon luggage into the overhead compartments, then buckling into their seats, engines can be heard as they're started one at a time, while one of the forward flight attendant closes the exit door with one of the desk agents checking to make sure the door is sealed and secured, locking it from the outside. The attendant gives a sharp rap on the outside of the door, acknowledging all is secure from the outside. As the engines begin to rev up, there is a thump as the tow barge pushes the Airbus A350 away from the aerobridge, until the plane comes to a stop, you hear the engines power up as the aircraft begins moving along the flight line before reaching the runway.

The flight crew consist of Captain James Easterson Jr. with First Officer Loretta Parker. Captain James Easterson, "Tower, requesting clearance for take-off, BA1 *235*."

JFK Tower, "BA1 *235*, you are cleared for departure, runway zero-nine."

Captain, "Roger, tower, clearance for departure, runway zero-nine, BA1 *235*."

Captain to First Officer Loretta Parker, "Okay Loretta, we got the go."

Captain, "Tower, BA1 *235*, rolling, we are clear. Cheers!"

It's an 11-hour 51-minute flight to Heathrow International Airport. Captain Easterson made the mistake of having one too many sodas before boarding, now has to make a quick pit stop before nature gets the better of him. The captain turns to his first officer, telling her that he's got to hit the rest room or else there will be a very wet cockpit in no time flat. First officer, "When you got to go, you got to go!"

Captain calls for Nancy Houston, senior flight attendant, letting her know that he needs to leave the cockpit to use the lavatory.

First Officer, "No problem, sir, I got this one. Watch for turbulence while you're in the lav."

Captain Easterson leers back at Loretta exclaiming, "Ha-Ha funny!"

Captain, returning to the cockpit, asks his first officer for a favor. Captain, "Loretta, remind me to only have one small soda with lunch, okay?"

First officer, "Yes, sir!"

In the meantime, three young men are seated in business class where they have been watching on who leaves or enters the cockpit as they converse in their native tongue. They are Omar Sultan, Khalil Aman, and Shah Nasir. Omar, lead terrorist, will not make any kind of move towards the cockpit because it is going to be a very long flight. He is contemplating that when either the captain or first officer is served lunch, it'll be the ideal opportunity to rush the cockpit door and take over control.

Six hours into the flight, Captain, "Loretta, would you like to have lunch?"

First Officer, "Yeah, I think I should. I didn't have much of a breakfast this morning."

Captain, "Okay." Captain picks up the phone calling Nancy at the front attendant serving station.

Captain, "Nancy, would you come into the cockpit to take Loretta's lunch order."

Nancy knocks on the door as she has been instructed to alert the captain and first officer that someone from the flight crew is on the other side of the door. First Officer, presses the door release button, unlocking it allowing Nancy to step into the cockpit. Nancy walks over to Loretta, asking her what she wants for lunch. Nancy writes down Loretta's lunch order telling her, "I'll be back with your lunch in a half hour."

The three men in the business class seats watch intently as they confer on how they will synchronize their rush into the cockpit. A half hour has passed as Nancy stands outside the cockpit door; she proceeds to call the Captain on the phone by the security lock panel. While she is on the phone, Omar, and Khalil approach the cockpit door, as the door opens, they push Nancy into the cockpit following close behind. Both the captain and first officer are caught unaware that these two men have managed to sneak in taking control of the cockpit. Omar asks Nancy to place the lunch tray down, leave the cockpit immediately, say nothing to no one. Captain, "What do you want?"

Omar, "We need the use of your plane."

Captain, "For what purpose? What are you going to do? Kill me and my first officer, hijack the plane, crash it into a mountain or a skyscraper full of people?"

Omar, "No, Captain. You and your First Officer should consider yourselves very lucky today. We have no plans on killing you, your First Officer, crew, or the passengers. We need you and your first officer alive so you can fly the plane to Fayzabad Airport in Afghanistan."

132

Captain, "*Afghanistan!* Why?"

Omar, "When we finally land in Fayzabad, the passengers will be asked to get off, a large group of our soldiers will get on, then you will fly us to Incirlik Air Base in Adana, Turkey."

Captain, "What are you going to prove by your actions."

Omar, "That we are capable of carrying out our objectives and will not let anything get in our way."

Captain, "You know that when we land in Turkey, all of you will be targeted by Turkish and U.S. military troops. Most of you might be killed."

Omar, "We know the risk. If some of us manage to survive, we will head into the highlands, try to make our way back to Afghanistan's friendly towns and villages that support our cause."

Captain, "Okay, I have your word that the passengers and flight crew will not be harmed in any way, *right?*"

Omar, "Allah as my witness, I swear to you no harm will come to anyone aboard this plane."

Captain, "Okay, when it's time, I'll make the course change to Fayzabad Airport."

Omar, "Thank you, Captain. I am sorry it has to be this way."

Captain, "It's a cause that you believe in."

Captain Easterson with First Officer Parker continue on their scheduled flight plan. Captain Easterson begins to contemplate on just how truly lucky both he and his first officer were not to be killed. Typically, in a hijacking scenario, terrorists are compelled to execute the crew in order to gain full control of the aircraft. The Captain, intrigued by such a diametrically opposed choice allowing them to live, he had to probe deep into the mind of one of them to find out why. Captain turns back to his right as he looks down at the floor as Omar sits cross-legged with his hands cupped in prayer. Captain, "Omar, it'll be a while before we have to change course, would you mind if we talked?"

Omar, "I find that to be quite unusual, Captain."

Captain, "Why do you say that?"

Omar, "When hijackers commandeer an airliner, the last thing you would expect is for the flight crew to start a casual conversation with those that have disrupted normal life putting everyone onboard in peril."

Captain, "Well, let's try. We're not going anywhere other than where the flight plan takes us."

Omar, "Alright, Captain, let's try."

Captain, "What makes you and those that follow the calling different from other terrorists, whose objective is always to kill the flight crew then using the aircraft as a weapon of destruction."

Omar, "Not all of us, in what you call the Middle East, are born and raised to be terrorists and murderers. Many of us have loving parents that work hard sacrificing much to provide a better life for their children, to teach us to be good people, honor family, marriage, love our children, follow the holy teachings and doctrines of the Quran. We have aspirations and dreams like everyone else. We wish better for our children in the hopes that they exceed the sum of their parent."

Captain, "Well, I see that no matter what part of the world you're from, the goals for parents towards their children is no different from anywhere else."

Omar, "I know of many that I grew up with, taking passages from the Quran twisting them to satisfy their own inadequacies by killing and destroying those that were different from them. This must give them a level of superiority over others, as they prepare for the day when they will make the ultimate sacrifice, giving up their lives in Jihad, in the name of Allah to combat evil and sin they see all around them."

Captain, "Why don't people like you try to explain to the world that not all of you think and act the same?"

Omar, "That would be a fantasy, Captain, to think that people like me can convince the rest of the world that there are actually good terrorists that don't wish harm and destruction to others. I'm sure that they would view what I'm doing right at this moment, as a wrong and terrible thing."

Captain, "If you manage to pull this off today, you show that no one onboard this plane was killed, the flight crew was not eliminated, airplane not destroyed, shouldn't that raise an eyebrow for many as a good gesture showing that not all of you are nothing more that senseless unfeeling monsters?"

Omar, "Perhaps, Captain, but many, many of you must be watching while listening to the message in order to be understood."

Captain, "I will try to make my voice be heard so others will begin to understand that you cannot judge a race of people merely by the actions of a bunch of segregated, misguided nonconformist."

Omar, "Your words hold promise that many of us may finally be vindicated, not to be categorized as murderers and terrorist."

Captain looks over at the elapsed flight clock realizing that it's time to make the course change as he told Omar he would. Captain and First Officer prepare to input the new course heading for the Afghanistan border. After the new course change, everyone in the cockpit notices a blinking red light on the T.E.O.S. control panel. Omar immediately questions the Captain on why that light is blinking.

Captain, "To be perfectly honest, I don't know why it's blinking. I'm not completely familiar with all the functions. I have yet to use the onboard T.E.O.S., system so I'm not sure what that light indicates."

Omar, "Are you still in control of the airplane?"

Captain, "Yes! we'll continue flying and let's see what happens."

After ten minutes, the blinking red light turns solid red, there is still no change in aircraft controls. First Officer looks out her starboard window noticing the air inlet doors around the engine nacelle opening. Suddenly, the whine of giant electric motors can be heard. The first officer looks out again noticing that the air intake for the starboard engine is closed off. Captain Easterson turns to his port side window noting that the engine to his left is closing as well. Immediately, the power levels for both engines drop to about 15-20% of full power. Another set of electric motors begin to wind up, power is increased to about 55-60% of full power. Omar, "Captain, why is this happening?"

Captain, "My only explanation is that T.E.O.S. has detected some weakness or flaw in the primary engine systems, it's now trying to compensate so engines don't stall."

Omar, "Do you think that we can make it to Fayzabad?"

Captain, "We're not running on full power but we have more than enough power to make it to our destination. The system has stabilized and we're still up and flying, can't ask for more. I should contact Heathrow letting them know of our current status."

Omar, "Captain, I ask that you don't contact anyone. Please continue on the course heading you are on, get me to where I need to be."

Captain, "Alright, I'll comply."

Hours later, the British Airways flight is five miles out ready to begin final approach to Fayzabad Airport. Captain, "Tower, this is British Airways *235*, we have an emergency situation that requires priority clearance to land."

Tower, "What is the source of the emergency, British Airway *235*?"

Captain, "This flight has been commandeered by a terrorist group. Their intentions do not seem to be hostile, but ask that no one on the ground interfere with them or passengers will be hurt."

Tower, "For the sake of all the passengers and flight crew, we will not alert authorities or the military."

Captain, "Thank you, there is to be no bloodshed. These terrorists do not mean anyone any harm, let's keep it that way."

Tower, "Affirmative, we will keep everyone at distance."

Captain, "Thank you, I will relay that to our captures."

Tower clears all incoming flights into the airport giving flight *235* priority clearance to land. After arriving safely at Fayzabad Airport, T.E.O.S. is successfully reset, engines back to full power again. Omar and Khalil exit the cockpit as they prepare to open the forward fuselage door. Khalil looks out from a first-class window as he watches one of his brethren pulling up in a mobile boarding stair truck positioning the stair center to the exit door. The driver gets out of the truck, proceeding up the stairs, knocking on the door to let Omar and Khalil know that he will help open the door from the outside. Omar stands in front of the cockpit as he yells to all the passengers to grab their belongings then quickly exit the plane. Passengers begin to question each other on why such an unusual request comes from the cockpit. "We need everyone to quickly exit this plane. Please don't ask any questions, just do as we ask." Passengers gather their things walking briskly as they exit. One passenger stops asking Omar about their luggage in the hold. "Do not worry, your luggage will be returned to you undamaged."

As all the passengers and non-essential crew members are allowed to deplane, the waiting terrorist soldiers board the plane taking any seat they can get in to, the captain asks senior flight attendant Nancy Houston to secure the forward exit door before proceeding. Captain and First Officer prepare for takeoff, but check with the tower for final takeoff clearance.

Captain, "Tower, British Airways *235*, requesting final clearance for takeoff."

Tower, "British Airways *235*, you have final clearance for takeoff. All incoming air traffic has been placed on a holding pattern until you are airborne."

Captain, "Thank you tower for all your help and understanding on this matter. Please make sure that all the passenger and the rest of my flight crew are well taken care of."

Tower, "British Airways *235*, we will take good care of passengers and crew. Safe trip, Captain."

Captain, "Thank you, tower, British Airways *235*, has clearance and we're rolling, Cheers!" Captain and First Officer setup on the runway as they push the engine throttles to full take off power, aircraft rotates with a new flight plan now taking them to Incirlik Air Base, Turkey.

As British Airway *235* lines up on final approach for the air base, Captain calls the tower, warning them that the flight is not scheduled to land there but has been compromised to do so by terrorists onboard. Tower, "British Airways *235*, we cannot guarantee that ground military forces will not storm the aircraft when it lands."

Captain, "I'm going to ask a very unconventional request from you. Can you divert the military from rushing the aircraft until all the terrorists have left? I don't want a giant firefight breaking out around the aircraft should a stray bullet end up piercing a wing tank causing the aircraft to catch fire then explode."

Tower, "We can try. We see your point very clearing."

Captain, "Other than the cockpit crew, along with two flight attendants there are no passengers onboard, they deplaned in Afghanistan."

Tower, "Alright, Captain, we will try to take as much attention away from the plane once you have landed."

Captain, "Thank you, tower. Please have all other air traffic cleared, we're about to land."

When the plane lands in Incirlik, front and rear exit doors are opened, emergency chutes deployed, allowing all the terrorist to quickly slide down to the tarmac. They run into the foothills surrounding the air base as they take up defensive positions for what may come. Omar, Khalil, along with the one terrorist seated in business class, Shah, are standing by the left side front emergency chute as they prepare to exit. Omar instructs his friends to jump, he will be close behind. Omar, "Thank you, Captain. You will be remembered."

Captain, "May your God guide you in your quest to seek equality."

As he turns quickly to slide down the chute, Omar yells out, "May Allah be praised!"

Moments after the last of the terrorists run into the foothills, a squad of military jeeps and troop carriers surround the plane as Turkish soldiers position two mobile boarding stair trucks at the front and rear exit doors. Two soldiers come running into the cockpit.

"Where are the terrorists?"

Captain, "They managed to flee into the hills minutes before your forces arrived."

Chapter 12

Joe arrives unannounced at R&R Industries, steps up to the
security desk, asking to see Ryan Comfort as he identifies
himself. Security guard picks up the phone, dialing Ryan's
office extension. Ryan picks up, guard notifies him that Joe
Sherman is here to see him. He replies to the guard that he
would be right down to escort Joe to his office. The guard
hanging up the phone, tells Joe that Ryan would be down
shortly. Joe thanks the guard as he places an ID badge on
his shirt then sits down to wait. Moments later, Ryan exits
a main lobby elevator as he walks towards the front
reception area. Joe stands up, shakes Ryan's hand then is
asked by Ryan to follow him. They get to Ryan's office; Joe
ask that Ryan close his office door.

Joe, "Ryan, I had to come to see you to ask if you heard
about the recent incident that happened on a flight from San
Diego to Heathrow airport?"

Ryan, "No, Joe, to be honest, I didn't hear anything
about it."

Joe, "Oh man! Glorious, just fantastic!"

Ryan, "Okay, Joe, don't keep me guessing!"

Joe, "When I tell you, you'll be very happy. It was a
British Airways flight bound from San Diego International

to Heathrow International; somewhere during the flight, a group of terrorists hijacked the airplane."

Ryan, "Did they kill the flight crew, then taking control of the plane?"

Joe, "*No!* Believe or not, apparently these terrorists didn't know how to fly an Airbus A350. They needed the flight crew alive so they could commandeer the plane, then have it land in Afghanistan."

Ryan, "*Afghanistan!*"

Joe, "Yeah, you heard right! Their plan was to have all the passengers and non-essential cabin crew get off the plane when they landed. A large group of Islamist guerrilla fighters known as Mujahideen would get onboard to be flown to Incirlik Air Base in Adana, Turkey."

Ryan, "What was that going to prove?"

Joe, "The lead terrorist claimed that by doing this, it would prove to the Turkish and American military that as a small band of independent guerrilla soldiers, would be able to easily infiltrate any enemy positions."

Ryan, "Does anyone know what happened to them?"

Joe, "According to the captain and first officer that witnessed it all, the soldiers exited the plane by deploying both emergency chutes, sliding down quickly as they ran into the foothills surrounding the air base. Not certain if there were any casualties, but they did manage to prove their point."

Ryan, "That was a daring plot on their part. How about T.E.O.S.?"

Joe, "*Oh damn!* I can't believe that the most important part of this whole story nearly eluded me. T.E.O.S. worked exactly as Cody said it would. When the course change was made, T.E.O.S. sent the acquisition signal as it was supposed to. The air inlet doors began to open, the shielding blade assembly closed off, the air injection unit began blowing air into the engines. The captain and first Officer noted that engine power was only about 50% of nominal until they landed. System was reset before taking off again. Now I hope that the government never finds out what we did or it won't be good for anyone of us."

Ryan, "The system worked, Joe! Plane didn't crash, no lives were lost, I consider it a win-win scenario."

Joe, "Yeah, this time. I just wish we can eliminate the terrorist equation without having to involve T.E.O.S. I just want it to work as I designed it."

Ryan, "Keep the faith my friend. You'll never know what the future holds for the fate of terrorism."

Joe, "Ryan, is Cody around? I'd like to give him the great news and a big ass bear hug!"

Ryan, "Sorry, Joe. Cody took a couple of days off because he and the wife are celebrating their tenth wedding anniversary."

Joe, "Good! He deserves some time off to celebrate with his wife. Thanks to him, hopefully no more crashes because of T.E.O.S. When he gets back, give him my best, share the great news."

Ryan, "Will do, Joe."

Joe gets up from his chair as he opens Ryan's office door, He stops, saying, "Okay, while I'm here, is there anything else we can do to make T.E.O.S. even better than what it is?"

Ryan replies, "We can try."

An Air Force C-17 Globe Master III is dropping off needed supplies and equipment for the Antarctic research center at the southern tip of Ross Island. After three hours of unloading all necessary supplies and equipment, a blizzard not thought to be a threat sweeps through the southern part of Antarctica, creating a severe white out condition forcing all aircraft to be grounded for the rest of the day. United States Air Force Lt. Major Maxwell (Max) Logan was concerned that having the aircraft sit overnight in sub-zero temperatures would make it difficult for engine start up; most of the lubricants in the engines would be nearly frozen. If by the next morning, the blizzard subsided, it'd be necessary to defrost the engines enough to where all lubricated parts could run without causing damage to internal engine components, allowing the C-17 to take off from McMurdo. Lt. Major Logan asked the ground support crew on how many aircraft ground heating units they had available. Replying that they only had two units available. The C-17 having four engines, would take much longer, only doing two engines at a time. Once the first two engines were defrosted, they would need to be started, kept running until the other two engines could be started. Lt. Major Logan turns to his First Officer Captain Perry Addams for advice on getting the engines warmed up. Lt. Major Logan, "Perry how are we going to do this? Then be able to get the heck out of here quick?"

First Officer Captain Addams, "Sir! Don't you remember, this C-17 is specially equipped with not only the T.E.O.S. system. Pratt and Whitney also added internal heating elements inside the air injection units. This will produce hot intake air necessary to keep engine components from freezing in this type of weather."

Lt. Major Logan, "You are absolutely right, Perry. I can't believe that I forgot about that."

Captain Addams, "No problem, sir. Anyone of us can get frostbite on the brain in this climate," he mildly chuckles, as not to insult his superior officer.

Lt. Major Logan, "Okay, this is what we're going to do. About two hours before we take off, we'll get a GPU (ground power unit) hooked up to the C17. Run T.E.O.S. as we normally would in emergency mode then turn on the heating elements to force hot air into the engines. After two hours, we'll try start up on number 1 to see if it runs smoothly."

Captain Addams, "Great, Major. Sounds like a plan."

Dr. Franklin! Dr. Franklin, is Elli back from the Ross Ice Shelf? Dr. Nelson Franklin, "No, why?"

Gerry Hathaway, research assistant to Dr. Elli McPhenson, "Elli left just at the break of dawn. She was going to get fresh ice samples from the Ross Ice Shelf. She was going to use one of the Snow cats to get to the edge of the ice shelf, then trek to a spot she has marked on her GPS that has given her very good data results from samples collected previously."

Dr. Franklin, "About how long ago was that, Gerry?"

Gerry, "Well, Doctor, being that we're in the summer months, the sunlight doesn't set, my best guess is that she left at about five o'clock in the morning."

Dr. Franklin, "What time is it, Gerry?"

Gerry, "It's after twelve in the afternoon, local time."

Dr. Franklin, "How long would it normally take for Elli to get to the spot where she normally goes out to, get her samples, then return back?"

Gerry, "Six hours tops."

Dr. Franklin, "Okay, give her another hour, in case she decided to take additional samples enough to meet her research requirements."

Gerry, "Very well, Doctor. If she's not back by then, do we form a search team to go look for her?"

Dr. Franklin, "Definitely, something must have happened, she could be hurt or unable to call in."

An hour passes, Gerry starts to mobilize volunteers willing to go out to search for Dr. McPhenson. Along with Gerry Hathaway, five other volunteers from the station join him in the search for Elli.

They arrive at the spot where the doctor parked the Snowcat to continue trekking to her favored ice shelf location. The six researchers are securely tied together with safety ropes between them making sure no one falls through a crack underneath the snow. As they near the GPS spot known by Gerry as the place Elli normally gathers samples from, they begin calling out her name hoping she's conscious, she will be able to answer loud enough for the group to hear her. They call out her name, then wait about fifteen seconds to hear a respond, should she be weak with not much strength. They continue calling, then they wait. All of a sudden, they hear what sounds like a very faint distance reply to their callings. They call out her name again, then wait. One of the members in the group hears Dr. McPhenson's voice. They continue listening hearing her voice echo a little stronger. They continue walking finally coming up to the edge of a crevasse. One of the members calls out her name, then they gratefully hear her say, "I'm down here, I'm hurt. I think I broke my left arm, and right leg. I'm cold, my fingers are frostbitten."

One team member, Jim Gears decides he's strong enough to climb down the crevasse, get to the injured Dr. McPhenson, helping bring her back up. The members rig lowering ropes, anchoring it with their ice axes. When Jim gets to the injured doctor, he takes one of the lowered ropes securing it around the doctor's waist.

Jim, "Okay, I'll let you know she's got a good grip on me and we're ready to ascend. Pull us up slowly, remember the doc is injured, she only has one good arm."

Jim, "Okay, pull us up." Jim cautiously maneuvers from one side of the crevasse to the other, trying to find the best way up without accidentally smashing Dr. McPhenson's body onto a ledge that would cause her to lose her grip from Jim's jacket.

About forty-five minutes go by, as team members see Jim's safety helmet as he nears the top of the crevasse, he grabs one of the ice axes, pulling himself up until the other members can get a good hold on Dr. McPhenson, being careful not to injure her even more. When Jim and Elli are away from the edge, Jim is out of breath, stressed from trying to bring Dr. McPhenson out of such a narrow passage. Immediately, Gerry Hathaway calls McMurdo station for a rescue helicopter to come pick up the injured Dr. McPhenson. Half hour later the helicopter arrives. Two rescuers exit bringing with them a rescue basket. They loosely splinter both Elli's left arm and right leg, then carefully place her inside the basket, cover her with blankets, carrying her over to the helicopter. They secure the basket, proceeding back to McMurdo station to evaluate Elli's injuries and frostbitten fingers. After the helicopter lands at McMurdo station, Elli is immediately brought in to see the base doctor. She is brought to an examination room, then placed on a table. The medical staff scrupulously cut as they remove the doctor's jacket, slicing open her thermal suit to expose a broken right leg. First thing the base doctor discovers that Dr. McPhenson has an open fracture below the knee at the tibia. He then moves over to Elli's left arm, as he notices that the left arm has multiple breaks at the humerus. He instructs his staff to clean, sterilize, cover the wounds as he heads towards the office of Dr. Franklin, the acting director of the research facility.

Doctor John Evans, the base doctor proceeds to explain to Dr. Franklin that Elli's injuries are too severe to be treated at the McMurdo station. He strongly urges Dr. Franklin that Elli must be transported to a hospital in Australia. They would be better equipped to treat both the open fracture on her right leg, and the multiple breaks on her left arm. Dr. Franklin agrees with Dr. Evans evaluation of the injuries, calling a hospital in Melbourne to ready a room for Dr. McPhenson, who will be transported as soon as possible. The problem that still remains would be getting an air ambulance that could arrive quickly enough to transport Dr. McPhenson so her injuries will be taken care of before getting worse. Dr. Franklin remembers that a United States Air Force C17 was already at McMurdo and could easily transport Dr. McPhenson to the hospital in Melbourne. Dr. Franklin calls Gerry Hathaway into his office asking Gerry if the crew of the C-17 would transport

Elli to the hospital in Melbourne. Gerry, "I'll ask doctor. I'll find out where the pilot's quarters are, then ask them if they could transport Dr. Phenson to a hospital in Melbourne."

Gerry inquires around the base, is told where he can find Lt. Major Logan and his First Officer. Gerry arrives at the temporary quarters of the C-17 flight crew to ask about transporting Dr. McPhenson. Gerry finds their quarters, then knocks. First Officer Captain Perry Addams answers the door. Captain Addams, "Yes, can I help you?"

Gerry, "Yes, sir, I truly hope so."

Captain Addams, "What is it you need?"

Gerry, "Sir, we have an injured researcher that fell about sixty feet down a crevasse while taking ice samples from the Ross Ice Shelf. She has multiple breaks on her left arm and an open fracture on her right leg below the knee. The base doctor doesn't have the equipment at the hospital to take care of these injuries. She would need to be transported to a hospital in Melbourne."

Captain Addams, "I'll talk to Lt. Major Logan. I don't see why we couldn't do that for someone at McMurdo station."

Gerry, "Thank you, sir. When you decide, you can get in touch with the director of the research station, Dr. Franklin. He can then make sure Dr. McPhenson is ready to travel to Melbourne. Thank you, sir."

Captain Addams, "Your welcome, it's our duty to help all those in need."

Captain Addams confers with Lt. Major Logan as he agrees that it's important to get Dr. McPhenson the medical attention she needs before her injuries become much worst. Lt. Major Logan arrives at Dr. Franklin's office to discuss with him how Dr. McPhenson is to be prepared before transporting her onboard the C-17. Lt. Major Logan, "Dr. Franklin, it's very important that Dr. McPhenson's injuries be well packed and insulated so any bouncing she experiences onboard the aircraft will not make her injuries worst."

Dr. Franklin, "I understand completely, Major. You let me know when you're ready to leave, I'll make sure Dr. McPhenson is secured in a rescue basket once she is on the plane."

Next morning, three hours before scheduled take off, the pilots instruct the runway ground crew to hook up a Ground Power Unit (GPU)to the C-17 to bring power to T.E.O.S., to start defrosting all four engines simultaneously. The air inlet doors opened, the shielding blade assembly closed, the air injection unit with heating elements turned on, now they wait.

After three hours, temperature sensors located by the turbo fan assemblies located after the T.E.O.S. air injection units show temperatures have risen to about 39 degrees Fahrenheit. Major Logan ask First Officer Captain Addams to start engines. First Officer Captain Addams, "Yes, sir, Starting engine 1. Engine is beginning to spin up, igniters on, fuel on, we're good. Starting engine 3. Engine spinning, we got combustor flame."

First Officer Captain Addams repeats the process for engine 2, then finally for engine 4. All engines started, running at normal values. Lt. Major Logan, "Perry, let me go tell Dr. Franklin they can get Dr. McPhenson ready to transport."

Captain Addams, "I'll keep the engines at a higher idle so any components not yet up to temperature will reach standard operating equilibrium."

Lt. Major Logan, "Pat the old lady on her behind, tell her to keep the kids singing."

Captain Addams, "Aye, skipper."

Lt. Major Logan exits the C-17 through the open rear cargo door walking across the frozen tarmac to the research building to have Dr. Franklin prepare Dr. McPhenson for travel. Lt. Major Logan knocks on Dr. Franklin's open door, "Okay, Doctor, we got all engines singing loud. Is the patient ready to travel?"

Dr. Franklin, "Yes, she is. I anticipated that the Air Force would be two steps ahead and be ready for us."

Lt. Major Logan, "Working up here in this freezer, we have to be ready for anything."

Dr. Franklin, "Major, we'll bring Dr. McPhenson out to the plane."

Lt. Major Logan, "We'll be waiting for her."

Two of the researchers, one on either side of the rescue basket bring Elli through the rear cargo door of the C-17, then hand her over to waiting airmen that strapped the rescue basket to an aluminum framework securing Elli for the trip to Melbourne. Both researchers say goodbye to Elli, wishing her luck, then they both exit as the massive rear cargo door begins to close finally locking giving a green "*go*" light. Lt. Major Logan, "McMurdo, this is Air Force cargo *5143* requesting clearance for take-off."

Tower, "Air Force cargo *5143* you have clearance for take-off, proceed when ready."

Lt. Major Logan, "Tower, ready for take-off, Air Force cargo *5143*."

Tower, "Affirmative, good travel and our best regards to your passenger Dr. McPhenson."

Lt. Major Logan, "Roger, tower, thank you, I'm sure Dr. McPhenson will appreciate that much. Air Force cargo *5143* clear."

T.E.O.S. got all four engines on the C-17 Globe Master III to successfully start for takeoff from McMurdo Sound on Ross Island, Antarctica. Takeoff was successful as Dr. Elli McPhenson's injuries were attended to, as she now can rest comfortably in a Melbourne hospital.

Chapter 13

It's a typical early hot summer evening in Las Vegas with temperatures reaching over 105 degrees. Many of the passengers waiting to board are exchanging their fun experiences while in Las Vegas. Some of them were wishing that they didn't have to go home. For others, the casinos had no sympathy for those that decided to play the craps table or blackjack. The flight crew this evening consists of Captain Stewart Kilpatrick along with First Officer Danny Smith. All passengers have boarded, aircraft is towed back from the aerobridge, pilots have started both engines, plane is under its own power as it moves along a side apron along with a fleet of other airliners forming a conga line, as they all await their turn for take-off clearance. Finally Spirit flight *1666* prepares to turn on to the runway to be given clearance. Captain Kilpatrick, "Tower, requesting clearance for take-off, Spirit *1666*."

McCarran tower, "Spirit *1666*, you are cleared for departure."

Captain, "Roger, tower, clearance for departure, Spirit *1666*."

Captain to First Officer Danny Smith, "Okay, Danny, let's punch it!" Captain, "Tower, Spirit *1666*, rolling, we are clear."

It's a 4-hour 42-minute flight to Dulles International Airport. Over 2 hours into the flight, somewhere over Missouri some passengers looking out their windows noticing a very ominous storm front extending from left to right, being at least hundred miles wide.

Passengers notice repeated flashes of lightning coming from deep within the super cell, some of them comment hoping that the flight crew will try to find a way of flying around this super storm. Meanwhile, back up front in the cockpit, both Captain Kilpatrick and First Officer Smith are also aware of the impending super storm as they now try to decide whether to fly through or go around. Captain, "Danny, what do you think? Go through or try to fly around?"

First Officer, "It's going to be a bear to fly through this thing, Captain."

Captain, "Danny, what's our fuel reserve?"

First Officer, "If we try to go around it, it will eat up most of our fuel reserves. We'll be lucky if we can request an emergency landing to refuel before pressing on."

Captain, "Any other ideas?"

First Officer, "We can try a lower altitude, but we have to watch for microburst."

Captain, "What is Doppler showing?"

First Officer, "So far, no sign of microburst activity. There is a lot of electrical disturbance."

Captain, "Okay, let me call the tower at Kansas City and let them know that we'll drop down to twelve thousand feet then try to ride out the storm until we clear it. We'll climb back up to our original altitude after."

First Officer, "Sounds good, sir. I'll watch the Doppler for any sudden changes with this storm system."

Captain Kilpatrick, "I'm calling the tower."

Captain, "Tower, this is Spirit *1666*, requesting altitude change to angels twelve, to avoid flying through super cell."

Tower, "Spirit *1666* we have you on radar, request noted to reduce altitude to angels twelve. Advise if altitude is to change again."

Captain, "Roger, tower, reducing altitude to angels twelve. Will advise after clearing storm."

Tower, "Affirmative, Spirit *1666*. We will keep you on radar. Good luck, be safe."

Captain, "Thank you, tower. We're just about into the mouth of the dragon. Spirit *1666*, we're clear and praying."

First Officer, "Ready, Captain? May be a rough flight."

The captain announces over the PA that he has reduced altitude to twelve thousand feet and will try to fly through the storm until it is safely behind us. He explains to the passengers that trying to fly around the storm would consume too much fuel, there would be a need to land in order to refuel. The captain announces that everyone keeps their seat belts on. Not to be out of their seats in case of extreme turbulence. Captain Kilpatrick and First Officer Smith begin to carefully maneuver the A321 into the mouth of the storm. Fifteen minutes into the storm, the airplane comes upon an area of the storm highly electrically charged with several very large lightning discharges streaking around. Suddenly, a massive bolt of lightning hits the A321's starboard wing, all the lights in the passenger cabin as well as the cockpit momentarily go dark. After a few seconds, the lights return but are flickering. In the cockpit, control systems are fading in and out. Captain Kilpatrick tries to restart the APU for auxiliary electrical backup, but that also fails. Some of the flight instruments have blacked out with some being air speed indicator, altitude indicator, engine power indicators. Then it happens, the complete electrical system onboard the airplane fails, everything goes dark. Both engines stall, losing all power. The A321 starts to quickly lose altitude, the captain makes the decision to send out a mayday.

Captain, "Damn it! The radio is probably dead; hell with it, I'll try anything. *Mayday! Mayday! Mayday!* Spirit *1666*, severe lightning strike, all electrical systems dead, both engines have failed, rapidly losing altitude. Will attempt to keep aircraft in the air for as long as possible. Engine restart failed; we are a 'dead stick.' Danny, if you can see through all this rain, see if you can find somewhere to land this bird, now."

First Officer, "I'll try, sir. I can't tell how high we are and how fast we're going. I guess we'll find out real quick."

Captain manually unlocks the cockpit door, runs out yells out to the flight attendants to brace for impact. Flight attendants quickly yell out over and over, "*Brace! Brace! Brace!* For impact."

A moment later: *Crash…*

Two hours after the crash of Spirit Airlines flight *1666*, both television and cable news stations interrupt their normal programming to report on the latest breaking news about an airliner crash. Opening logo opens ups for KMBC-TV channel 9 in Kansas City, Missouri, as the camera does a close-up pan on the news anchors, the camera turns to one gentleman seated to the left as he shuffles his papers in order to begin speaking. "Good evening, everyone, I'm Jack Colbert with my co-anchor Sid Philips. We start our news report tonight with a very terrible airline tragedy occurring over the skies of Kansas City. At about 6:37 this evening, an airliner, Spirit flight *1666*, as it was flying through a very severe super cell, was, as some believe struck, by a super bolt of lightning, causing the aircraft to lose all electrical power, mechanical engine functions, causing the aircraft to become what aeronautic expert term as a "dead stick." The aircraft ended up crashing in an open field near the town of Columbia, that happens to lie between Kansas City and St. Louis. There were no reports of ground dead or injured at the site where the airliner crashed. KMBC-TV has dispatched a television crew to survey and report from the crash site. Camera pans over to Sid Philips as he announces that the ground crew at the site is now setup and ready to report. Ladies and gentlemen, we will now switch you to our KMBC-TV field reporter Jacque Sandberg standing by."

Sid Philips, "Jacque, can you hear us here at the station?"

Jacque, "Yes I can, Sid. As my cameraman pans the area of where the airliner crashed, it's very evident that no one could have survived and walked away from this."

Jacque, "The only fortunate part to this tragedy is that no one on the ground was anywhere near when the airplane crashed."

Jacque, "Someone that is here at the site told me that an eyewitness saw when Spirit flight *1666* crashed in this open field."

Jacque turns to a local standing to her right as the cameraman pans over to get the man's face into the view of the camera. Jacque, "Good evening, sir. Did you happen to witness when the airliner crashed?"

Junior Simson, local farmer whose property was just about a mile away from the crash site. Junior, "I happened to step out into the front porch of my home, as I looked up into the tempest filled sky, I saw the airplane falling out of the sky, very fast and when it hit the ground the sound of the impact was tremendous. The plane burst into flames with several explosions following. I got in my pickup heading as fast as I could over here."

Jacque, "When you arrived, sir, did you happen to see anyone else at the crash?"

Junior, "No, ma'am, no one else."

Jacque, "Thank you, sir. I won't keep you any further."

Junior, "Thank you, young lady. I will pray for the families that lost their loved one from this disaster."

Jacque, "Thank you, I hope that your words will somehow bring a small degree of comfort to those that have suffered and endured such great loss." Camera pans back to focus on Jacque's face as she is ready to sign off on her report from the crash site. Jacque, "This is Jacque Sandberg, KMBC-TV reporting from Columbia, Missouri returning you now to the studios."

Sid Philips, "Thank you, Jacque, for your insightful report of Spirit Airlines flight *1666*. We will now return you to regular programming in your area."

Two days after the crash of Spirit Airlines flight *1666*, news stations from around the country report that one of those onboard the flight was United States Congressman Neal Albert Karina, republican from Washington D.C.'s Park View ward. He was killed along with his wife June with their two children Todd and Lisa returning from Las Vegas. Congressman Karina was a very well respected and notable politician that fought hard for the rights of low income and senior groups throughout many impoverished neighborhoods across the country. It has also been found out that while the investigation of flight *1666* is still underway by the National Safety Transportation Board (N.T.S.B.), the Federal Aviation Administration (F.A.A.) has mandated all service maintenance logs on the aircraft from Spirit Airlines. After the F.A.A. studied the logs it was found that some months before the aircraft was taken out of service to make major repairs to the starboard wing, removing it in order to replace structural members that were suspect to fatigue according to F.A.A. service inspections. Some aeronautical experts trusted by the F.A.A. were given copies of the inspection reports, they concurred as did F.A.A., that it's very possible that by disassembling the starboard wing from the fuselage, by the time the wing was to be re-assembled, there could have been a slight misalignment that might have caused the super lightning bolt going past the sealed opening between the fuselage body and the main wing mounting members. Experts believe that as the lightning hit the starboard wing, instead of travelling across the top of the wing then exiting to the back of the aircraft, the charge found a large enough gap between fuselage and wing supports allowing it to go into a main electrical distribution trunk as it travelled in both directions. Aft towards the Auxiliary Power Unit (APU) shorting all control and distribution circuits. Then travelling forward shorting out primary, secondary, and tertiary systems, gravely affecting all of the cockpit and passenger sections including electrical and cabin pressurization systems. More details will become available as the investigation intensifies its search for more conclusive evidence.

It's morning as Joe receives an early call from Ryan Comfort. Ryan, "Hi, Joe, this is Ryan. How are you?"

Joe, "Okay, how are you?"

Ryan, "I'm fine, I guess."

Joe, "What's the reason for your call, Ryan."

Ryan, "Joe, I need you to come to R&R Industries. There is something very important that I need to discuss with you."

Joe, "Is it an emergency?"

Ryan, "Sort'a, but I need you to be here so I can discuss it face to face."

Joe, "When do you want me there?"

Ryan, "At your earliest convenience."

Joe, "Okay, I'll hop a flight, see you tomorrow."

Ryan, "See you then."

Joe, "Are you alright, my friend? You sound kind of down."

"I'll see you tomorrow. Bye."

As Joe walks up to the front of the R&R Industries building, he notices that the second American flag and the company logo flag were at half-staff. He never gives it a second thought as he continues to walk through the main entrance. Joe identifies himself to the guard at the desk, guard calls Ryan informing him that Mr. Joe Sherman is here to see him. After Joe has checked in with the front security getting his ID badge, Ryan steps out from one of the main lobby elevators, walking towards where Joe is sitting. Joe stands, extends his hand, shaking Ryan's hand. Ryan ask Joe to come upstairs to his office. Joe enters the elevator, as the door closes, he looks over at Ryan, notices that Ryan has a blank and distant look on his face. They exit the elevator walking towards Ryan's office. Ryan gestures to Joe that he'd walk in first, closing the door to the office behind him. Ryan, "Thank you for coming, Joe, on such short notice."

Joe, "Not a problem. I told you a long time ago that I'm always here for you guys."

Ryan putting his head down as he is going to speak, "This is going to be very difficult to tell you. I'm not even sure I'll be able to keep it together to get my words out," Ryan's voice begins to crackle.

Joe, "Tell me, Ryan. Don't hold back, my friend, what's wrong?"

Ryan, "Cody and his wife Vicky were killed on Spirit flight *1666* out of Las Vegas."

Joe lays both hands flat on Ryan's desk, he puts his head down on top of his hands, after a short pause, he raises his head. Raising both of his hands as he cups both his eyes as he starts to sob uncontrollably then slams his hands down on Ryan's desk yelling out, "No, damn it, why? why?" Joe, with tear filled eyes as they ran down his cheeks. "He was my friend, a colleague, an incredible soul I respected and looked up to. He was the one person responsible for transforming T.E.O.S. from being a rogue killing machine to a benevolent life saver. It can now protect, yet stops terrorists from killing and destroying the innocent. I'm going to miss him so much."

Ryan, "I'm sorry I had to call you in to give you the terrible news."

Joe, "Oh, Ryan, if you didn't, I would have hated you if you would have kept this from me."

Ryan, "We were all very close to Cody. He was a great guy, an electronics and computer whiz, what he left behind can never be duplicated. Are you feeling any better, Joe?"

Joe, "Yeah, I'm glad I didn't have my emotional outburst in that open-air conference room the next floor above."

Ryan, "I would have had to tell everyone on the floor that you didn't like what I ordered for lunch!"

For a brief moment, Joe's sadness turns to laughter as Ryan joins in to help relieve the pain that was still felt inside both men.

Ryan, "Joe, we're going to have an impromptu memorial that will be held in the main auditorium in about half hour. The CEO along with the vice president of research and development will be there to speak to everyone as they say some words about what kind of person and employee Cody was. Joe, would you like to say something in memory of Cody?"

Joe, "Yes, I would. I will be honored to speak to everyone about Cody. You know and I know that without him, the monster would still be much live. Of course, the part of how he altered the programming can never be divulged."

Ryan, "Good, all of us are grateful for your contribution to R&R Industries, whom better than you to speak?"

Ryan and Joe walk into the auditorium from a back-entrance door as they walk on stage taking one of the seats positioned behind the podium before the memorial begins. First, the CEO for R&R Industries greets everyone, then talks about the amazing contributions left behind by Cody. Then, the vice president of research and development speaks about what an incredible asset, Cody was to the whole of the company. Ryan gets up from his chair, as he walks to the podium to introduce the next speaker. Ryan, "Ladies and gentlemen, most of you know him and have seen him here at R&R Industries for many years and has become sort of a permanent fixture within the company. Without any further delay, my friend Joseph A. Sherman."

Joe gets up from his chair as he extends his right hand to shake Ryan's hand as Joe takes hold of Ryan's right lower arm with his left hand. Ryan pats Joe on the back as he returns to his chair. Joe gets close to the podium, clearing his throat before he speaks.

Joe, "Good morning, ladies and gentlemen, and distinguished company representatives. This is not going to be easy to talk about who and what Mr. Cody Banks meant to me and I'm sure to everyone else here. How can you gauge a person's worth and contributions when no matter what you say, it can never be enough to truly exemplify such an extraordinary individual, I must consider myself extremely fortunate to have worked with such a brilliant and sometimes enigmatic individual, never really knowing who he was. Cody was never one to totally lower his guard. He was generous to a fault with his advice and knowledge, but he always kept the best for himself. He was someone that possessed greater understanding, yet there was an innocence that drove him to the curiously level of a child always looking for something new, something greater than the sum of all that he was. I can continue here talking for hours, but what would it accomplish? Cody will live in my heart, I'm sure he will live in yours. Thank you for your time in listening to me. I feel that I must end this before I get a stern warning glare from the CEO as he reminds me that you people have to go back to work."

The audience chuckles and some lightly clap.

Joe, "Thank you very much."

Many of the audience stand clapping as Joe goes back to his chair, sitting down as he waves to the audience.

Chapter 14

Joe arrives at the headquarters of the National Transportation Safety Board (N.T.S.B.). Joe arrives unannounced and will not leave until he gets answers that will satisfy his queries. He must somehow venerate the life of his friend Cody and his wife.

Joe walks through the front entrance of the National Transportation Safety Board as he approaches the front reception desk. The young lady at the desk turns her chair to face Joe. Joe leans over the counter to get a better look at the young lady smiling up at him. Joe, "Hi, there. My name is Joseph Sherman and I'm here to see Mr. Jackson Elliot. I was hoping to talk to him about any details he could share with me about his investigation on Spirit Airlines flight *1666*."

Receptionist, "Oh, I'm so sorry, Mr. Sherman, Mr. Elliot is not currently handling that investigation. Mr. Henry Boyd is the lead investigator for the Spirit flight *1666* crash."

Joe, "Would it be possible for me to see Mr. Boyd on such short notice?"

Receptionist Shelley, "I'll ask Mr. Boyd if he can make the time to see you."

Joe, "Thank you, I would appreciate the chance to meet with Mr. Boyd."

Shelley, "If you will excuse me, I will go talk to Mr. Boyd. He's in his office, it's just down the hall. I'll be back in a few moments with an answer."

The receptionist leaves her desk, stops at a corner desk nearby the reception area, to ask if someone could watch her desk while she went to talk to Mr. Boyd. Another young lady gets up from her desk then walks towards the receptionist desk. A few moments later, the first receptionist is heard walking back towards the main reception desk. She thanks the second receptionist, then getting up returning to her desk. Shelley turns to Joe who was sitting waiting for an answer; she tells Joe, that Mr. Boyd will make time to meet with him. She motions to Joe to come up to the desk so she can issue an ID badge for Joe to wear. After Joe puts on his ID badge, the receptionist asks him to follow her to Mr. Boyd's office. Joe and the receptionist approach Mr. Boyd's office. Shelley turns to Joe as she introduces Mr. Boyd to Joe.

Shelley, "Mr. Joseph Sherman, I would like you to meet the assistant director of the N.T.S.B., Mr. Henry Boyd."

Joe, "Thank you very much for all your help in getting Mr. Boyd to meet with me."

Shelley, "You're very welcome, Mr. Sherman. Have a very nice day."

Joe, "You as well."

Joe steps into Mr. Boyd's office as Mr. Boyd stands to shake Joe's hand. Mr. Boyd, "Mr. Sherman, it's a pleasure to finally meet you. Please have a seat."

Joe, "Thank you very much, Mr. Boyd. Are you currently in charge of the investigation of the Spirit Airlines *1666* crash?"

Mr. Boyd, "Yes, I'm in charge of the crash investigation for Spirit flight *1666*. How may I assist you today?"

Joe, "I would like to make sure that the N.T.S.B. is going to do everything possible to get to the bottom of this terrible disaster."

Mr. Boyd, "We are still only in the preliminary stages of this investigation; have yet to determine the exact cause of the crash."

Joe, "Is there anything substantial you can tell me at this time?"

Mr. Boyd, "We are still sifting through every single piece of wreckage to clearly define what happened."

Joe, "So, at this time, nothing you can tell me? Mr. Boyd, please understand that I lost a very close and dear friend on that flight and it will be hard to put his memory behind me that quickly."

Mr. Boyd, "I understand completely, sir, I'm very sorry but I have nothing at this time. I'm sure that he meant a lot to you. I promise I will do everything within my power to get to the truth about this crash. Here is what I can do Mr. Sherman, I can invite you to the hearing that will be held when all the evidence has been collected, and a final report published that will be made available to the public along with the F.A.A."

Joe, "YES! I would like that very much, to attend that public meeting."

Mr. Boyd, "Consider it done. Leave your email and cell phone number at the front desk, we will make sure to contact you with a date and time."

Joe, "Thank you, Mr. Boyd. Thank you for everything. Have a nice day."

Mr. Boyd, "You as well Mr. Sherman."

Joe, "Thank you."

Joe arrives back at his hotel room, then quickly calls wife Tracy to let her know that the N.T.S.B. has nothing to offer at this moment. But they will let him know when the public hearing is to take place, where he is to be invited to attend. Joe showers, then goes downstairs to grabs a quick bite to eat at the hotel restaurant. He returns to his room, packs his bags, goes back down to the front desk as he checks out. As Joe waits for a cab outside the hotel, he's in conversation with one of the hotel patrons having a light and carefree dialog considering the terrible consequences he has been made part of within the past couple of weeks. As Joe looks towards the circular entrance road in front of the hotel, he spots a cab just as the cab is about to pull up to take Joe to the airport a black SUV pulls up cutting off the cab before it has a chance to stop. The cab driver gets out of the cab yelling and waving his hands as he walks towards the driver side door of the black SUV. A few seconds later, the cab driver is walking backwards still looking at the SUV apologizing for his rude and loud behavior promising that it would not happen again. Joe just watches as the drama unfolds in front of him. The rear SUV passenger window opens slightly, a voice from the back seat is heard saying to Joe, "Mr. Sherman, please step into the front passenger seat."

Joe thought to himself, *I've heard that voice before.* He steps in, closes the door, the SUV drives off. Voice from the back seat, "Good evening, Mr. Sherman. How have you been?"

Joe, "Mr. R., I presume?"

Mr. R., "You are correct, Mr. Sherman. We know why you're here in Washington. We know of a very close and dear colleague of yours from R&R Industries was recently killed along with his wife on a flight heading back from Las Vegas. I don't want to seem cold and callous, but this time we had nothing to do with it, nature is a much greater force than even the United States government."

Joe, "So, Mr. R., what is the reason for this impromptu meeting?"

Mr. R., "We just wanted to make sure that all that is, is still the same. We like to keep track of persons of interest."

Joe, "So, I have become a person of interest? Are you and your operatives becoming worried that I'm going to take this incident and denounce the federal government, saying they did it? So, your covert government agency can then try to clear itself of any wrongdoing."

Mr. R., his voice hesitant, but still direct, "Yes, something like that. The thought did cross the minds of some of my associates."

Joe, "No, sir! This time it's personal. I need to know. Just out of curiosity, have you or your associates ever felt any kind of remorse for the deaths of all those people onboard Delta Airlines flight *4502*? I understand that the plane was hijacked by terrorist and their intentions were not honorable as they were going to crash the plane into the U.S. Capitol Building. It's still my wish where T.E.O.S. could be used for the purpose it was intended for. Somehow hinder the terrorist ability to use the plane as a weapon of destruction without the plane being forced to crash killing everyone onboard."

Mr. R., "Well, Mr. Sherman, sounds like a very noble proposition, but terrorists know what they need to do when they're in control of a situation."

Mr. R., "Well, Mr. Sherman, we have arrived at the airport. Have a safe flight."

Joe, "Well, until the next encounter."

Mr. R., "I'm sure of it. Good night, Mr. Sherman."

Joe, "Good night. Oh! I see you knew what airline I was flying."

No response from the back seat as Joe steps out from the SUV. As the vehicle drives away, Joe just stares at it until it rounds a corner, then disappears.

It has been five long months since the crash of Spirit flight *1666* bound for Dulles International airport that crashed somewhere near Kansas City Missouri, due to a severe super cell with heavily charged lightning. The aircraft had a manifest of two hundred seventeen passengers, a total crew compliment of seven, including the captain and first officer. The N.T.S.B. has completed its final report revealing the findings in their investigative report to both the public and the F.A.A. A month before the scheduled public hearing, Joe receives a confirmation from Mr. Henry Boyd of the N.T.S.B. to come to Washington to be present at the hearing in regards to the Spirit flight. On the scheduled day, Joe walks into the conference room where the hearing is to take place, looks around, spots a table near the front where the N.T.S.B. panel will be seated.

Joe walks towards the table, pulls out a chair, sits down placing his briefcase next to his left leg.

Joe was hoping that no one would sit next to him. He was not in the mood for idle chit chat. He was there on a mission to learn why his friend Cody and his wife needlessly perished that day. All the panel members from the N.T.S.B. take their seats at the front of the conference room where all the evidence complied will be heard by both the public, airline officials, aeronautic experts, and members of the F.A.A. Mr. Henry Boyd seated in the middle of the panel members, adjust his microphone as he is about to speak. Henry Boyd, Lead N.T.S.B. investigator, "Ladies and gentlemen, members of the media, distinguished pilots, airline officials, and members of the F.A.A. I thank you all for being here, I will now go over all the investigative results on the crash of Spirit flight *1666*. The plane crash occurred in an open field within the small farming town of Columbia, which is situated between Kansas City and St. Louis, Missouri. The captain of the Spirit flight was given clearance from Kansas City Air Traffic Control to reduce his altitude to twelve thousand feet. We have been able to obtain this information from Air Traffic Control communication transcripts. As investigators sifted through the debris wreckage, they found both the flight data recorder, and the cockpit voice recorder, it was evident that the super lightning bolt short circuited all electrical systems onboard including both of the boxes. There was no information that could be extracted. The communication logs show that Captain Stewart Kilpatrick attempted to navigate through the storm without having to circumvent around the storm cell since the matter of fuel reserves was of significant importance…"

While the N.T.S.B. public hearing was in session, Ryan Comfort walks in, scans the room noticing Joe Sherman sitting at a table towards the front near where the N.T.S.B. panel members were seated.

Ryan makes his way over to where Joe is sitting. When he gets to where Joe is at, Joe has his head cupped in between his hands, he is slumped forward, seemingly out of it. Ryan pulls the chair out next to Joe's left. Ryan sits down, then bumps Joe's left arm with his right hand, Joe slowly lifts his head from his hands, turns, as he looks at Ryan. Ryan, "Hi, do you attend these functions often?"

Joe, "Only if they're serving New York cheesecake with sour cream topping for lunch," as Joe pauses for a moment. "I hate being here, Ryan. You saw that I was holding my head up. I was so deep in thought, imagining the last minutes that Cody and his wife had before the plane went down. I would give my right arm if T.E.O.S. would have been able to protect that plane from the lightning strike."

Ryan, "Joe, if every single gadget ever designed to protect planes was installed. It would look like one of those old *Monty Python* cartoons where everything including the bathroom tub was part of an airplane."

Joe, "You know, Ryan, this may sound like something out of the Bible, but every feeling in my soul tells me there was some kind of really bad omen associated with that flight."

Ryan, "Why do you say that?"

Joe, "Something about having six, six, six, in that flight number is disturbing. I can't help but think of the devil himself sitting on top of the fuselage coaxing the lightning to take its best shot at knocking down the plane."

Ryan, "I can't blame you for thinking that because we have been conditioned since early on to associate six, six, six, with the devil, Lucifer, Mephistopheles, or whatever other name it goes by."

Joe, "I guess I'm just making too much of it. I'm trying to find an un-holy excuse why that plane crashed."

Both men compose themselves then continue to listen to the details of the hearing.

Henry Boyd, "…By using most of the fuel reserves, this would have required the crew to land and refuel. The crash occurred on the evening of June 16, approximately 6:37pm. There were no survivors.

"It is believed that while flying through this violent super cell, an extremely large highly charged lightning strike hit the starboard wing of the aircraft. This is based on the evidence of charred discolored paint, where the lightning initially contacted the wing. The initial impact of the lightning was so severe that parts of the starboard wing have physical holes burned into the wing as though it was hit by some form of plasma cutter.

"We can only then speculate that the amount of energy that hit the wing was substantial enough to cut right into the exterior aircraft grade aluminum skin.

"The N.T.S.B. consulted both an aerospace structures and mechanical air frame engineer to approximate how the lightning hit was able to travel to the interior of the aircraft. They both inspected the wreckage concluding that there might have been a very slight misalignment between the fuselage support mounts by the starboard wing box which attaches to the main body section of the aircraft. This also confirms the service logs provided to the F.A.A. by Spirit Airlines. This slight misalignment or gap produced a conductive opening allowing the lightning to find an interior grounding source. Under normal circumstances, when a lightning bolt hits an aircraft, the lightning charge is deflected as it skims across the body of the fuselage exiting towards the rear of the aircraft. In the case of flight *1666*, when the lightning hit, it traveled pass the aircraft's exterior, hitting several cable bundles located close to the air frame cable conduits.

"Some of the shorted cable bundles, handled power coming from the APU (Auxiliary Power Unit). With all these wires being shorted, there was a total power disruption to the cabin and the cockpit. Both the flight and voice data recorders were completed damaged due to the lightning strike where no data could be extrapolated. Once the wiring was completely shorted, the flight systems became inoperative thereby causing engines to stall, the aircraft became what is known as a 'dead stick.' In closing, on behalf of all of us at the N.T.S.B., we would like to express our deepest condolences to all those that lost their loved ones. This was a very unusual disaster in where what would normally be expected to happen when lightning hits an aircraft during severe super cell storm activity. The fact that the aircraft, just months before, was serviced for reconstruction of structural support members. So when the starboard wing was reattached to the fuselage, a misalignment occurred but was not inspected closely enough to visually discern that the additional gap now present at the fuselage and wing joining, created a potential hazard as in the situation that occurred when lightning hit the aircraft.

"Ladies and gentlemen, I will turn you over to the Senior F.A.A. Director Mr. Samuel Cohen as this concludes the N.T.S.B. public investigation report."

Senior F.A.A. Director Samuel Cohen, "Thank you, Mr. Boyd, for now the F.A.A. is satisfied with the report and will consider this case closed unless new evidence can be produced to shed new insight on other causes for the crash. I would like to take a moment giving my personal reflections on this terrible tragedy. I believe that this unforeseen accident causing such total destruction of lives and property will now awaken new F.A.A. implementations for more stringent regulations and guidelines tailored to closer inspection procedures when aircraft must be serviced before being put back into full flight status. It's imperative that no aircraft be allowed to fly unless a full mandatory inspection is issued with proper certifications and signatures. Thank you, ladies and gentlemen."

Henry Boyd, "Thank you, Mr. Cohen. Ladies and gentlemen, this now concludes the public hearing on the crash of Spirit Airlines flight *1666*. Thank you."

After the hearing, both Joe and Ryan get up from their chairs, leaving the N.T.S.B building. Ryan, "Joe, you want a get a bite to eat?"

Joe, "Yeah that sounds good. Believe or not, I'm hungry as hell."

Ryan, "Great, I know of a little outdoor cafe that serves a mean corn beef and pastrami sandwich. It can rival that of Katz's Deli in New York City."

Ryan hails a cab as both men get in the cab to grab a bite to eat at the local outdoor bistro Ryan suggested.

Chapter 15

This year a vast area of the country's northeast has already seen above average snowfall amounts. Vermont has been one of those states logging in totals making travel out and about a difficult trek. This is due to changing weather patterns attributing to the aggressive precipitation that has fallen so far. A local air service company out of Newport Vermont, Savin Air Vermont Express (SAVE) will be flying vitally needed parts for three of Qantas Airline's Boeing B747's out to Brisbane, Australia; as soon as parts are manufactured and ready to be shipped from a local Vermont aerospace company. Due to the large amount of snow and ice storms in the area, the local aerospace company charged with the task of producing the much-needed parts had suffered a major setback. Two nights prior during a very intense ice storm, the main electrical lines were snapped off from the nearby power pole. Utility crews were not able to restore electrical service to the company due to very treacherous conditions making travelling out to repair the site ill-advised. It was two days after, that utility crews were able to begin repairs restringing electrical lines back up on the pole. By the following morning, power was fully restored allowing machinist, welders, floor assemblers to resume their scheduled workload in the shop. After only a delay of three days, parts were finished, then carefully shrink wrapped, insulated, then crated for shipping. Parts arrived promptly as Northeast Kingdom International Airport where parts were off loaded onto a modified Airbus A350 cargo transport, as they were made ready for the long haul to Australia. On board are Captain Jake Lewis, First Officer Marty Simmons with flight engineer Doug White. Along for the ride are cargo masters Cy Newman, and John Gormley. Everything is loaded, secured, ready to go. The flight will be over eight thousand four hundred nautical miles, taking about a day and a half to complete. The following morning, the Airbus A350 is ready for takeoff, current weather conditions are reported favorable all the way to Brisbane. Captain Lewis, "Northeast tower, SAVE *03* requesting take off clearance."

Tower, "SAVE *03*, proceed to runway three-six and hold. One heavy on approach. You are next in line."

Captain, "Roger, tower, will hold."

Incoming aircraft lands, SAVE *03* is given clearance.

Tower, "SAVE *03* you are cleared for takeoff."

Captain, "Affirmative, tower, cleared for takeoff, runway three-six, SAVE *03* rolling."

Savin Air Vermont Express rotates off the runway, now on route to Brisbane Airport, Australia.

…In other news from around the world, terrible monsoon weather has hit the Solomon Islands causing severe flooding in many of the small outlying islands, there is also the threat from rising tide waters. An urgent plea comes from some of the local orphanages in the Solomon Islands. Local people of the area are afraid that between the rising tides with heavy rains, some of these orphanages may be washed away. These buildings are near rivers which have been known in past years to crest, flooding to dangerous levels.

The pleas from these orphanages finally gets the attention of Washington where the call goes out for any charity air services that would fly to the Solomon's to save as many of the children in the area since they have no parents or family that can claim them, only those that take care of them, along with only having each other. A champion to the cause emerges to let the world know that it will take on the challenge to save as many of the children from the Solomon's before they become endangered. Savin Air Vermont Express (SAVE) is that champion. As soon as the announcement is made public, many aerospace service companies hear about Savin's unselfish deed to help. Some are ready to donate fuel and maintenance services required to make certain the SAVE A350 flying the mission will have what it needs to successfully complete its task. In a surprise announcement, Australia offers its closest airport from the Solomon Islands, Brisbane Airport, to help with the efforts. They also added that refueling and maintenance services involved with the mission can be setup at the airport. Additionally, local food and apparel companies chime in, offering their services to help the children as well. Many other companies from as far away as Europe and the far east have already given their commitment to help as well…

Back home in Vermont at Northeast Kingdom International Airport, CEO and president of Savin Air Vermont Express, Paul Savin calls an emergency meeting with his staff on how they're to proceed with the rescue mission. Paul Savin, "Okay, guys, can we do this with just the A350 that's on its way down there?"

Sid Bloomberg—Flight Ops Manager, "Well, sir, it's the only one available that can make this happen. We have the 737 but it doesn't have the range of the A350."

Paul, "What else?"

Sid, "That's it, sir. The other aircraft are Gulfstream, Lear and Embraer's."

Paul, "Did the A350 get a full checkup before it left?"

Sid, "Yes, sir! it was in the maintenance hangar for about a week. It was touch and go there for a while. Turns out when Andy, our F.A.A. mechanic was looking over the engines, Andy spotted a small leak coming from the number 2 engine fuel distribution manifold. We did have an available replacement in-house. The unit was swapped out, unit was pressure tested, but it failed by the time the F.A.A. inspector was ready to sign off. Unit had to be removed, then both the mechanic and inspector noticed a slight irregularity to one of the input nipples on the manifold that was allowing fuel to leak out even when the line was attached securely. Had to run the manifold back to our aerospace vendor where they had to completely disassemble the manifold and machine a completely new body then reassemble it again, air pressure tested it in their water testing tank. Manifold held good pressure, got it back to the mechanic re-installing it, did additional pressure testing getting a clean bill of health from the F.A.A. inspector."

Paul, "Okay, after all that, let's keep the A350 as the primary. In case any of you were wondering why I'm doing this to save those orphans is because, I was an orphan.

"I was taken care of and raised in one of the orphanages here in Vermont. This may sound pretty much cliché, like out of an old black and white movie, but I got dropped off at the orphanage's front door, becoming their latest little bundle. The only thing that saved me as I was growing up was getting adopted by an incredible set of parents. They gave me a great education while teaching me about the importance of business. As an adult, I was fortunate to meet people in the aerospace industry that got me interested in starting my own air freight business. By making very sound investments in the market I was able to start this company. So now it's my turn to give back.

"It's something I usually don't talk about so what's in the past, stays in the past."

Sid, "I never knew! That's great! Thanks to your head for business, we all have jobs. Is there anything else you need to discuss with us, sir?"

Paul, "*No*, I believe everyone knows what to do. Thank you all."

A day and half later, the cargo laden A350 has come halfway around the world, now is about to land at Brisbane airport, Australia. As Captain Lewis and First Officer Simmons are nearing final approach, they both spot dark masses of clouds seen far off in the distance, just to the northeast of Brisbane. The captain and first officer know that this is what they must expect as they fly out to the Solomon's to start the rescue mission for the children. After the A350 safely landed, it's directed over to an unloading and staging area where replacement parts for three Qantas Airlines B747's will be unloaded. Cargo masters Cy Newman and John Gormley help direct the ground workers from Qantas to carefully unload all the parts getting them over to the Qantas repair hangar.

Afterwards, the captain, first officer, and flight engineer taxi the A350 to a service hangar, setup to house the plane while routine maintenance is performed before the plane can be cleared to continue onto its very important rescue. As the plane is being serviced, captain and crew decide they need a good eight hours of sleep before pressing on. An hour after both Jake, Marty, and Doug turn in for several hours of much needed sleep, a series of knocks are heard on the door of the pilot's lounge. Marty immediately gets up to answer the door. He opens the door, a mechanic in gray overalls stands in front of the door, as he's still wiping his hands with a shop rag. Marty, "Yes, can I help you?"

Mechanic, "Hello, mate, my name is Noah; I'm the mechanic that's working on one of your A350 engines. I got some bad news and some good news. The bad news is that you have a main fuel distribution line on your number 2 engine that is leaking. The good news is that I happen to have a replacement line in the shop that I was able to reconnect."

Marty, "Is every fine now on the number 2 engine?"

Mechanic, "It is. I did manage to do a preliminary pressure test. The line held pressure with no leaks anywhere. The only problem now is to get an aircraft inspector from the Civil Aviation Safety Authority to come out to sign off on the repair. They won't let you take off until an inspector for C.A.S.A. is made aware of the repair and will sign off allowing the aircraft to resume full flight status."

Marty, "How long with that take? As you know, we have to fly out to Guadalcanal on a rescue mission to pick up orphans there."

Mechanic, "That won't be a problem mate, my brother-in-law is a C.A.S.A. aircraft inspector. He's the guy that got me the job here at Brisbane Airport. Anyway, if he doesn't do this, all I have to do is make a call to my sister, you understand?"

Marty, as he laughs lightly, "I fully understand the power that a sister can have over a brother-in-law's way of thinking, Noah."

Mechanic, "I'll get back to the hangar, and call my brother-in-law. I'll get him here in a flash."

Marty, "*Thank you!* You are truly a lifesaver."

Mechanic, "Your welcome, mate. Bring all those children home safe."

Marty, "That's a promise, Noah."

Marty extends his right hand as he shakes the hand of the mechanic. Mechanic gives Marty a two-finger salute over his right brow, turning around as he heads back to the hangar.

News reports pour in that weather conditions in the Solomon's are rapidly deteriorating making rescue efforts even more perilous. An urgent call comes in from Paul Savin, asking Captain Lewis that his crew push on to getting the children as soon as the plane is made ready. Paul, "Jake, as soon as the A350 is ready to fly, it needs to be airborne."

Jake, "She'll be ready to fly within a few hours, skipper. Crews are working fast and hard to get her ready. I found out from Marty that we'll need an inspector from C.A.S.A. (that's the equivalent of the F.A.A. in the states) to sign off on all the repairs."

Paul, "Okay, Jake, you make the call when it's a go."

Jake, "Will do, thank you, sir!"

The following morning, the A350 is towed back from the service hangar, Jake, Marty and Doug go through preliminary flight checks, inputting coordinates for Honiara International Airport, on the main island of Guadalcanal into the onboard Flight Management System.

Jake, "Marty, are we ready to roll?"

Marty, "Just about, I'm going over all the fuel calculations with Doug to make sure we'll have more than enough in case we have to divert from our scheduled flight plan."

Jake, "Okay, guys, wrap it up as soon as you can so we can get going."

Marty, "Aye, Captain."

Ten minutes later, fuel calculations have been verified and inputted into the Flight Management System. Marty, "Cap, we're ready to roll when you are."

Jake, "*Great!* Go ahead and start the engines."

Marty, "Firing number 2 engine."

Engine begins to turn then the roar of the combustor igniting is heard. Then engine number 1 is started, when it reaches nominal idle speed, Marty lets Jake know. "Okay captain, all engines are hot."

As the A350 rolls down a side apron, Captain Lewis checks with his first officer on current weather conditions. Jake, "Marty, have you had a chance to check in with Brisbane Air Traffic Control meteorologist to get the latest updates for the weather conditions at Honiara International?"

Marty, "No, sir, not yet, but I will right now."

Tower, "This is SAVE *03* requesting weather advisories on conditions at Guadalcanal."

Tower, "SAVE *03* local conditions at Guadalcanal: High winds ranging from 30 knots per hour to gust as high as 50-60kph. Ocean with heavy chop, 4—6 feet with caps at 7—10 feet. Storm surge likely possible as strongest part of storm system nears Guadalcanal. Information from local tracking stations around the Solomon Islands indicate that seas are rough but still navigable. If any children from the outlying islands are transported by launch, extreme caution must be exercised to prevent capsizing of smaller displacement vessels. There should be little to no delay in getting out there quickly before conditions become too hazardous for a successful rescue."

Marty, "Roger that, tower. Thank you for the updates. Captain! It's imperative that we leave now!"

Jake, "Okay, Marty."

Captain, "Tower, this is SAVE *03* requesting takeoff clearance. Doug, keep a close eye on the engines for any sudden changes in performance. Need them running at 100% of full."

Doug, "Aye, Captain."

Tower, "SAVE *03*, proceed to runway zero-one, hold short."

Captain, "Roger, tower."

Tower, "SAVE *03*, you are cleared for takeoff."
Captain, "Tower, cleared for takeoff, runway zero-one, SAVE *03* rolling."

Tower, "Good luck, SAVE*03*, may the mission bring all the children back safely. Godspeed to you."

Jake, "Thank you, SAVE *03* out." The Airbus A350 rotates; now on its way to Honiara International airport. A three hour and fifteen-minute flight, no one exactly knows what they will face as they near Guadalcanal.

During the flight, Jake turns to his right as he asks Marty, "So, what happened with our number 2 engine."

Marty, "We ended up with a main fuel distribution line that was leaking."

Jake, "Boy, oh boy, that number 2 has been a real pain in the butt. What did the mechanic do?"

Marty, "He said that he had a replacement in the shop and was able to install it and pressure test it as well."

Jake, "I remember when I was drifting in and out of sleep, I thought I heard the mechanic say that the plane would need to be inspected by a C.A.S.A. inspector."

Marty, "You heard correct, skipper. Just like in the States, planes have to be signed off by an inspector just like the F.A.A."

Jake, "How did the mechanic manage to get an inspector so quick?"

Marty, "It seems that the C.A.S.A. inspector is the mechanic, Noah's, brother-in-law. Noah told me that if his brother-in-law didn't come out to do an inspection, he would make a call to his sister. She would convince him otherwise!"

Jake and Doug begin to laugh as both shook their heads in disbelief and relief. Jake, "Incredible! Gentlemen, so far, it seems as though nothing can keep us from rescuing those poor children. I guess this would be a good time to say, thank God. I'm curious, Marty, how is our fuel pressure holding out on number 2?"

Marty, "All levels are constant across both engines."

Jake, "Great, looks like the repair did the trick."

As the crew of the A350 nears Guadalcanal, cross winds are starting to buffet the plane around, captain and first officer are doing their best to keep the big plane on a straight course before crossing final approach markers.

Jake, "Marty, watch your heading. Whatever you do, don't let the plane start to yaw wildly. Between the cross winds and tail winds if we're not careful we'll end up landing one island over from Guadalcanal."

Jake, "Doug, watch the engines for any sudden power drops. We don't need a tornadic gust of wind flaming out one of the engines. Restart would be a bitch. We have enough on our hands besides dealing with engine restarts."

Doug, "Yes, sir. I'll watch for any fluctuations."

Captain, "Okay, boys! We're coming in. Gear down, flaps 15."

Marty, "Gear down, locked, flaps set at 15."

Captain Lewis and First Officer Simmons successfully land the A350 without incident. The weather has begun to get nasty. Rain and wind are whipping around making the rescue effort more difficult.

Chapter 16

Captain Lewis is instructed by Honiara tower to use the nearest service apron located close to the tower. They are to hold, while airport authorities have already been in contact with the orphanages that will be transporting children to the pickup area.

Children are being gathered from some of the small islands like: Malaita, Makira, Russel, and Florida. They'll be transported by US and Australian Coast Guard cutters bringing them to Guadalcanal.

These islands are the ones authorities fear the worst will be flooded by rising tides during this super storm. Some of the larger islands like Treasury Island, Vanuatu, and Isabel will have to be reached by the Australian Coast Guard. These ships are better equipped to handle the turbulent seas in the area, along with having greater capacity to carry more people.

Meanwhile, Captain Lewis is playing the scenario in his head of flying back these children to Australia, when he realizes that the A350 is a cargo plane with no passenger seats. The only seats found in the cargo hold are two jump seats for the cargo masters. How are we going to fit a hundred or even two hundred children and orphanage workers inside the belly of this flying behemoth with no place to sit.

Captain Lewis makes a request to Honiara tower if they can contact Brisbane Airport so he can talk to the airport director to find a way to seat all those children, so they can safely make it to Brisbane. The Honiara tower manages to patch a portable two-way UHF radio from the airport director's office, through the tower, so a link can be established to the cockpit communication radios in the A350. Jack Wilson, Brisbane Airport Director, "Captain Lewis. This is Jack Wilson. I'm the director of Brisbane Airport. I was told that you needed to talk to me?"

Captain Lewis, "Yes, sir, it's very important. I have a problem. I need to transport maybe two hundred or more survivors from Guadalcanal to Brisbane. I have nothing more than a giant cargo hold, with no seats. Those kids are going to be bounced around like beach balls in a romp room. I need to find someone local in Brisbane that can provide matting, mattresses, blankets, pillows, anything these kids can use instead of just sitting or lying down on a cold, hard, empty aluminum cargo deck."

Jack Wilson, "Alright, Captain. I'll make some calls. I'll let people know what you need to get these kids home safely."

Captain Lewis, "Thank you, Mr. Wilson. I have faith in you."

Jack Wilson, "I can promise you, sir! I will try."

Two hours later, a call comes in for Jake. It's Jack Wilson, from Brisbane Airport with some news.

Jack Wilson, "Captain Lewis. This is Jack Wilson."

Captain Lewis, "Yes, sir! Great news I hope?"

Jack Wilson, "*Yes!* I reached out to businesses using the power of local radio. A half a dozen bedding companies have offered to help with your plight donating hundreds of mats, child size mattresses, pillows, blanket, anything you need.

"Delivery trucks are arriving at the airport, as we speak, UPS (United Parcel Service) themselves have donated the use of one of their cargo jets to get what you need out to Honiara. As soon as the jet is loaded, the flight crew has been instructed to takeoff immediately; soon as the cargo jet lands, all bedding will be unloaded then transferred to your ship."

Captain Lewis, "How can I ever be able to thank you, the radio stations, those bedding businesses, and UPS?"

Jack Wilson, "Bring those children to safety. That's all everyone is expecting from you."

Captain Lewis, "That is my promise to everyone that has jumped in to help. Thank you!"

Jack Wilson, "You're welcome!"

Captain Lewis now waits the almost three hour and fifteen minutes it will take for a UPS cargo plane to arrive at Honiara International Airport from Brisbane Airport. It will all be worth it when the needed supplies to get the children settled into the A350 finally arrives. The A350 crew just anticipating for the children to arrive at Honiara Airport so they can be airlifted to Australia. Most of the children will be coming by launch send to the closest islands to pick them up. The islands farther away will be the responsibility of the United States Coast Guard, that has partnered with the Australian Coast Guard to help protect, keeping the waters around the Solomon's safe.

Twelve hours have already passed since Captain Lewis landed the A350 at Honiara Airport, just waiting for the children to arrive. The UPS cargo plane arrives at Honiara Airport, Guadalcanal. Crews from UPS, and the airport start to transfer all the supplies coming from Brisbane into the cargo belly of the A350. Both Captain Lewis and First Officer Simmons lend a hand helping to lay down matting and mattresses so the children will have somewhere to sit or lay down.

Two hours later, the SAVE A350 is fully loaded with supplies. From the back of the open cargo door, the inside of the plane looks like a giant slumber party romp room. Now, they just need the children. When the children arrive, they will disembark either at the Port of Honiara or Port of Noro. They will be shuttled by bus to the Honiara Airport, where authorities will do a quick head count making sure that every child and orphanage worker is accounted for. Captain Lewis and First Officer Simmons have been monitoring the long wave marine band on their shortwave for news about how the storm has intensified making the seas around the Solomon's even worst. Then comes the news of one of the launches sent out to Russel Island to pick up some of the children was hit by a rogue wave, capsizing the small craft. Reports coming in from the Coast Guard, report all the children on the launch were wearing life vest provided by both the United States and Australian Coast Guard. Luckily, within 20 minutes of the launch capsizing, all the children in the water were immediately rescued then transferred aboard an Australian Coast Guard cutter that was close by.

No lives lost, all children and workers accounted for.

During all this tragedy, a triumph shines forth like a beacon of hope. Finally, the buses start to arrive where the A350 is waiting, really for takeoff.

Captain Lewis and First Officer Simmons instruct the orphanage workers to get the children into the cargo hold quickly, help them find a place to sit down making sure none of them start walking around the cargo hold.

When the last of the children are onboard, Captain Lewis ask his cargo masters Cy and John to make sure all is secure and that everyone is hunkered down, prepared to make the flight. They close the cargo door, wait until the lock signal light goes green, the word is given to the flight crew that all is ready, they can proceed. Captain Lewis, "Marty, go ahead and start the engines."

First Officer Simmons, "Wilco. Starting engine 2…"

After engines are started running at nominal, the Airbus A350 taxies down the side apron, then waits for clearance from the tower. Captain Lewis, "Tower, SAVE *03* requesting takeoff clearance."

Tower, "SAVE *03*, you are cleared on runway two-four. Please be advised that tidal surges are starting to sweep across some of the coastal towns. Caution should be observed when taking off in the event of ground flooding along parts of the runway."

Captain Lewis, "Roger, tower, will observe standing water conditions during takeoff. Cleared for takeoff runway two-four, SAVE *03* rolling."

Tower, "Good luck, SAVE *03*, thank you for what you're doing. From all of us and for the children."

Captain Lewis, "Your welcome, SAVE *03* out."

As the A350 proceeds to roll down the runway, both the captain and first officer are watchful of standing water along the runway. As long as the airplane does not slide off the centerline of the runway, the captain and first officer will push the A350 as hard as it takes until it safely rotates becoming airborne.

At the last one hundred feet before the plane rotates, the A350 hits a large puddle of standing water, but at that point the front nose gear is light enough to where it skipped through the water, unaffected with just the main undercarriage landing gear feeling a slight shimmy. Finally, the plane rotated, now safely up in the air. The long trip back to Brisbane begins.

Captain calls back to the cargo hold, talks to cargo master Cy Newman. Captain Lewis, "Cy, everyone back there okay? Did the kids have a rough ride as we took off?"

Cy Newman, "Nah! These kids are real troopers. Some of them were even laughing. They liked getting bounced around."

Captain Lewis, "Boy! That's great. To be a kid again with no fear of danger. Cy, pass the word to all the workers that the children are not to stand or walk around during the flight in case of sudden turbulence."

Cy Newman, "Okay, Captain, I'll spread the word. The workers will make sure the kids are sitting or lying down."

Doppler radar is showing a massive storm front that will be too vast to fly around, it may be necessary to fly straight through it. Captain Lewis gives the order that if they hit ice or large hail, the T.E.O.S. system will be activated if it doesn't activate automatically as it should.

As they fly deeper into the storm, small hail pellets begin pelting the front windshield. As expected, T.E.O.S. system automatically activates as you hear the air inlet doors open, the air injection units starting, the shielding blade assemblies of each engine closing.

Now the flight crew is hoping that the hail will not get any bigger to where it could completely damage the windshield making visibility impossible. Obviously, nature does not follow any of the safety protocols that were expected. The hail increases to golf ball size with the frequency increasing. Just when the situation could not get any worst, the plane enters an area of the storm with tornadic turbulence, as it starts to buffet the aircraft violently. Captain Lewis, "Cy, it's getting really shitty out there. Make sure everyone is lying down, they need to stay down until told otherwise."

Cy, "Okay, Captain, everyone knows to brace for the worst."

The turbulence gets worst, some of the children start to cry. The workers onboard tell the older children to carefully crawl around the mat laden deck, to reach the younger children so they can be comforted by the older children until the worst part of the storm is over. Another twenty minutes go by, the worst part of the storm is now behind them. Captain Lewis, "Alright, Cy, I believe the worst is behind us now. Spread the word, it's starting to clear. Captain Lewis reaches over to the T.E.O.S. control panel, hits the override/reset switch, which shuts down the system returning engine operations to normal."

Within the hour, they will be landing at Brisbane Airport with a load full of rescued children. Captain Lewis instructs the first officer to go through landing sequence to make final preparations for landing. Captain Lewis, "Tower, this is SAVE *03* on final approach. Please have ambulances waiting in case any of the children or adults on board were injured during the flight."

Captain Lewis and First Officer Simmons line up the A350 making a perfect landing at Brisbane. Ambulances are already waiting at the airport by the time the A350 lands.

They open the cargo door, airport crews, the crew of SAVE *03*, with ambulance workers help the children and adults out of the plane. They're checked for bruises they might have sustained during the flight. Buses begin to arrive to shuttle the children with the adults to temporary shelters setup near the airport until its safe for them to return back to their homes.

The day after, a local TV reporter with Channel 7 Brisbane, tracks down Captain Lewis asking if he would do a live TV interview regarding the saving of all those children from the Solomon Islands.

Captain Lewis agrees but only under one condition. That his whole crew from Vermont, USA be present alongside him. The reporter agrees to it, the next morning the reporter meets with Captain Lewis with his crew. TV Channel 7, Brisbane Reporter, "G'day everyone, this is Samantha Gibbons with Channel 7 TV Brisbane reporting live from Brisbane Airport. Today we have the pleasure of speaking with Captain Jake Lewis, First Officer Marty Simmons, Flight Engineer Doug White, Cargo Masters Cy Newman and John Gormley.

"They work for Savin Air Vermont Express from the United States, who were responsible for flying to

Guadalcanal rescuing all those orphans that were in harm's way, airlifted from many of the large and smaller islands in the Solomon chain to Brisbane. This did not start out as a rescue mission, but it did in the end. Originally Savin, was to deliver replacement engines parts for three Qantas Airlines 747 planes needing repairs. It was the unselfish act of President and CEO of Savin Air Vermont Express, Paul Savin, that made the rescue mission possible giving the crew the go ahead to get the children and staff members from local orphanages. Let's go ahead, having the crew, in their own words, express how the events led up to a rescue effort.

"G'day Captain Lewis. Thank you for sharing your time in allowing our viewers to learn firsthand of your valiant rescue efforts."

Captain Lewis, "G'day to you, Samantha. We're all very honored to be recognized for what happened just one short day ago. I thought at first that it was going to be just a very long tedious flight from Vermont to Brisbane, delivering replacement engine parts. How events unfolded, to where the eyes of the world would now be watching all of us. Knowing that failing to rescue those children would have condemned all of us to a life of disgrace. Maybe my first officer can fill in the blanks where I might have missed something."

First Officer Simmons, "Thank you for this opportunity to tell the world how important it was for us to do this. I believe that each one of us made it his sworn duty to give it everything we had to succeed with our mission. It started and ended as a combined effort by all of us. We were all part of a collective that worked and thought as one. Without each one of us acting as a spoke within a hub, there would have been no wheel to help move us forward. That's pretty much it for me. Thank you."

Samantha with cameraman turn to the flight engineer, Doug White. "I'm not very good at this. I have always been better at reading engine and system gauges on aircraft, then composing my thoughts for an interview in front of a camera. All I can say is that we were all part of the same team, I had to make sure that I did my part, going beyond the extreme. Everything was extreme, for what we went through. I will say, this is pretty much it for me, as well. Thank you."

Samantha with cameraman turn to Cargo Masters, Cy Newman and John Gormley who were sitting together, maybe wanting it that way. Cargo Master Cy Newman, "Good morning, Brisbane Australia. You know, John and I normally don't get all this publicity back home. We're kind of the freight babysitters in the world of cargo logistics.

"But, boy! the load we had to bring back, we literally had to babysit our young cargo. When you deal with freight, if something gets loose or shifts, you just tie it down tighter. What do you do or say when a six-year-old that is being bouncing around in terrible weather, scared out of their innocent minds, looks up at you with tears in their eyes? You are totally powerless to make that bad old storm go away, helping to wipe those tears away. Well, that is exactly what happened when we were going through that very terrible storm, that I thought we were not going to make it. I have a young son and daughter back home close to the age of that one child. It made me do a lot of self-reflection, realizing that life is a commodity that is always fleeting. If we don't hold on to it tight, protect it anyway we can, it will slip right through our fingers being lost forever. I'm sorry." Cy rubbing his eyes, trying to keep the tears back, "I think that's it for me too. Thank you."

Camera pans over to John Gormley that was listening to his friend so intently that he himself was in deep thought. Samantha motions to John if he would like to add anything else. Cargo Master John Gormley, "I think that my associates have summed it up much better than anything I could add to this interview. I'm glad we did what had to be done, Thank you."

Samantha Gibbons, "Thank you, gentlemen. I'm sure that it has been an incredible ordeal, physically and emotionally. The way you now act and think must be somewhat different then before you got here a few days ago. I won't take up anymore of your time. I understand that tomorrow you're to depart back to the United States. I wish you, and I'm sure all the viewers watching across parts of Australia, the very best. A grateful thanks for what you have done, the lives that have been saved and touched by your unselfish and giving hearts."

Captain Lewis, "Thank you."

First Officer Simmons, "Thank you so much."

Flight Engineer White, "Thank you very much."

Cargo Master Newman, "Thank you. I learned a lesson that will stay with me forever."

Cargo Master Gormley, "Thank you. I work with a hell of a team, Uh?"

Samantha Gibbons, "Thank you, gentlemen. May you have a very safe, and uneventful flight home. This is Samantha Gibbons, TV Channel 7 at Brisbane airport. Back to you in the studio…"

Chapter 17

Joe tosses and turns in his hotel bed deciding he can't sleep anymore, why force it. He swings his legs across the bed to his left as he places them squarely into his bed slippers. He sits on the edge of the bed with his arms supporting either side of his body as he slumps over just staring down at his slippers. You hear a feminine voice yawning as she leans over laying her head on Joe's back still in a twilight sleep. Joe, "What's the matter, honey, you can't sleep anymore?"

It was Joe's lovely wife Tracy as she gently strokes Joe's back.

Joe, "I can't sleep anymore; today is going to be very hard on me. I'm nervous about giving a first-time commencement speech to a bunch of graduates that I'm sure are way smarter than me. Then talking about Cody and his wife will surely break my spirit if I don't strengthen up my emotions putting them in serious check."

Tracy, "You'll be fine, honey. During the speech if you feel like you're going to falter, just look out into the audience, look for me, I will flash you a smile to let you know all is well."

Joe, "Thanks, babe, that means a lot to me."

Before we go to the school, I need to stop at the cemetery where Cody and his wife are laid to rest. I got the address from Ryan Comfort for Westview cemetery in Blacksburg, Virginia. I have to pay my respects to both of them. I know it's going to kill me, but it's imperative I express my feelings to Cody and his wife before we continue on to the University.

Tracy, "Go, honey, you know you have to. If you don't, you'll never be able to clear your conscience that you didn't say what you had to say to your close friend and his wife."

Joe and Tracy arrive at Westview cemetery as they begin looking for the headstones of both Cody and his wife Vicky. After about a half hour of searching and asking one of the grounds keepers where they're grave marker were to be found, the keeper took Joe and Tracy directly to the resting site. Joe nears Cody's headstone, as he kneels with his right leg, brushing away the dead leaves laying on Cody and Vicky's grave markers. Joe places his closed right fist on his lips as he composes his thoughts before speaking. Joe, "Hello, my dear friend. Today I have been given the destined honor to speak in front of a graduating class at the same institution you graduated from. I'm sure that at some point and time, I'm going to think back at all that we did together at R&R and it's going to kill me. I'm so lucky to have my adoring and caring wife Tracy with me to help me get through all the rough spots I'll run into today."

As Tracy stands over Joe at the grave site, her head bowed slightly, she has a serious and distant look on her face. Both of her arms hang in front of her with fingers intertwined as though she's in prayer.

Joe, "Well, I got to get going my friend. If I happen to stutter for some reason, be there to give me a nudge so I can straighten up and continue my speech. I miss you and I will always feel that I lost someone very special to me. Goodbye, Vicky, keep this guy in line. Sometimes he was known to be a bit of a troublemaker. Good bye, Cody, rest in peace and maybe, just maybe, we can hook up again in the next plane of existence."

As Joe remains kneeling, Tracy's right hand presses firmly against Joe's left shoulder. He looks up noticing that Tracy has tears rolling down her eyes while looking down at him. Joe takes Tracy's right hand with his right hand getting up from kneeling, letting out a small sigh as his right knee cracks. Joe takes Tracy's right hand in his left hand as they slowly walk away. Joe stops as he faces Tracy, gently rubs the tears from Tracy's face with his thumbs. Looking at her Joe declares, "No more sadness today, I want us to be happy."

Tracy's response, "Yes, Joe, let's be happy today."

Joe leans over as he kisses Tracy on the lips beaming a big smile of admiration knowing she was there for him through a very sad moment. They continue walking pass the gates of the cemetery then to the car.

Joe and Tracy arrive at the main campus of Virginia Polytechnic Institute and State University. Joe locates the office of the Dean as he announces to the secretary who he is and his reason for being there. The office secretary looks at her clipboard, then looks up at Joe, smiles, then says, "We have been expecting you, Mr. Sherman."

She gets up from her desk saying, "Follow me, Mr. Sherman, we have a cap and gown reserved for this afternoon's event."

Secretary, "Here you are, Mr. Sherman. When the time draws closer, you may put on your cap and gown here, then I will escort you to the commencement stage."

Joe, "Thank you, you're most kind."

Secretary, "Don't mention it, Mr. Sherman."

Joe and Tracy take the opportunity to walk around the campus taking in all the sites and full history of the university. An hour before the commencement ceremony begins, a student is sent to bring Joe back to the main building where he is to get dressed in cap and gown. Joe tells the student to follow along as he finds a place for Tracy to sit during the ceremony. Joe, "Okay, honey, now that I know where you'll be at, I can spot you and look on you during the speech."

Tracy, "Okay, honey, I'm sure you'll give a great speech."

Joe, "Thanks, babe," as he kisses Tracy on her right cheek. Joe turns to the student saying, "I'm ready, lead the way."

Closer to the time, Joe is ushered to the steps of the stage. He is shown where he is to sit until he is called to give his speech. Joe walks onto the stage where all of the school faculty is gathered along with other invited guess. He takes his seat, then has light conversation with some of the faculty and invited guess. Finally, the commencement ceremony begins on time. First the dean does his opening speech, followed by other invited guess until it's time for Joe to give his speech. Joe rises from his chair, he steps up to the podium, wearing a ceremonial gown with mortarboard in the traditional Virginia Tech colors. Joe adjust the microphones, clears his throat, takes a quick sip of water, begins his commencement speech.

Joe, "I stand here before you as a man that has been humbled, yet strengthened by what life has given and lamentably taken away. With every triumph and tragedy, I have learned to master the outcome of each opposing faction."

Short pause…

"There is one very important reason why I agreed to be present to give this commencement speech today, or should I say special dedication? I wanted to share with all the graduating students, family, friends, esteemed members of this great university, what has been burning inside of me for some time now. I must release these emotions by philosophically expressing them to all of you."

Short pause…

"I came to find out that a very dear and close friend, that I collaborated with on the development of the Thrust Enabling Objective System was in fact a graduate at Virginia Polytechnic Institute. This incredible and remarkable soul was tragically taken from this world along with his wife Vicky on a flight coming out of Las Vegas. The couple were vacationing, while celebrating their tenth wedding anniversary. The plane was struck by a super-charged bolt of lightning shorting all the flight systems. This causing the plane to lose flight and navigational control as well as engine thrust resulting in the fatal crash that took place near Kansas City, Missouri."

Joe looks away from the podium for a moment, places his right thumb and pointing finger across the bridge of his nose. He clears his throat, takes a sip of water, then continues…

"I'm truly sorry for bringing up something so sad, then making it part of today's proceedings. Today must be a day of celebration and self-accomplishment for all of you that made it through every hurdle. I'm sure you sometimes felt downtrodden being ready to give up. As I look out among all of you today, some of you might be called upon to carry the torch of research and innovation that will light to blaze the way to a brighter future for all of mankind."

Short pause…

As Joe is about to speak, a commercial airliner cuts across the sky after taking off from Richmond International Airport. Joe looks up for a moment, gazing at the plane as it flies over the grounds of the campus. Joe looks back at his audience apologizing by saying, "I'm sorry, I have always had a fascination with aircraft of all types. It has been my love, my dedication to see planes become even safer. It's the reason for my obsession to design and create a system like T.E.O.S. I'm sorry again, please allow me to continue.

"My contribution to mankind has been quite different in comparison to the long years of study and sacrifice that all of you have made in order to be here today to receive your well-deserved laurels. Like a sailor or an explorer, I chose a course that took me in a totally different direction that may not have been exactly where I wanted to end up. I never regretted where I ended up. It gave me a chance to grow, intellectually, emotionally, to learn how to learn, to be challenged, to always rise above however circumstances presented themselves.

"I have been asked by many, if I ever went to college to complete my courses that would have earned me a degree in what I have loved the most, which is mechanical engineering. I feel I made excuses for myself in the past. Maybe I was scared, not of the hard work and commitment that lay ahead, but I was most afraid to fail myself, my wife, children, family, and friends. I don't think I could have ever really handled the self-humiliation."

Short pause…

Joe looks to where Tracy is seated, immediately noticing that his other very close and dear friend Ryan Comfort is sitting next to Tracy. As he looks at both of them, Tracy gives him a giant smile of approval as Ryan gives him two thumbs up. Joe composes himself as he continues his speech, "On the day that I was enlightened by an epiphany, I saw my invention come to life within my mind.

"On that day, my whole attitude changed because I felt that a force was driving my spirit to conceive a lifesaving system that would help protect and preserve human life and property.

"On that fateful day, I regained my worth as a man, on a mission to prove to myself, and the world that I could do anything, this time with no disgrace. As you embark from this great institution today, remember what impressed you the most to want to learn and excel to be the person that you have dreamt of since your younger days when deciding what to be, or do, as you became young men and women. Carry that enthusiasm and drive all through your lives in whatever you do. Make a difference, make a statement, leave your mark indicating that you were here. Never underestimate the power of one's self.

"Our lives are very short as measured on the clock of life—this is from a poem I read called *clock of life* as quoted by philanthropist Robert H. Smith. We sometimes can become arrogate, even careless, thinking that we have total control over our destinies, that we ultimately can determine when we have done enough or can do no more."

Short pause...

"There are no limits to what each one of us can accomplish. There can never be a preordained list of do's and don'ts that must be followed. Since our own lives have so many uncertainties, let your heart and mind be your guide to what is important, that holds a special and profound meaning for you. Remember, if you are a good person, then you will do what is good, it will then be recognized as a worthy accomplishment in the eyes of your peers."

Short pause...

"I anticipate that sometime in the future, I will be fortunate enough to meet, and work with some of you on a project that will help forge a long-time professional relationship like I had with my good friend Cody Banks. None of us are perfect. Maybe someday, man will have evolved into a being of greater compassion, understanding, love, and respect for one another. As for the world we live in, we must fiercely protect it, keep it flourishing. For now, it is our one and only true home. Don't do anything to destroy or deface the property, for the landlord will surely kick us out. I appreciate your kind attention while listening to my words. Hopefully, the meaning of these words will be clear to help inspire as well as guide you towards your yet predestined future.

"Until we meet again, congratulations, the best of luck to all of you. I thank you very much."

Joe waves to everyone in the crowd as people stand, cheer and applaud after Joe's commencement speech. As Joe is looking out to the audience, he bows his head as a performer would to acknowledge the accolades from the audience. Before he returns to his chair, Joe turns to shake hands with all those seated. Some of the faculty seated mention to Joe that they knew of Cody Banks, and were saddened to hear of what happened to him and his wife Vicky. In a sign of solidarity, Joe cups both hands around the hand of those faculty members that mentioned Cody and his wife. Joe just looked straight into their eyes shaking his head in disbelief with a blank expression. Joe turns, then walks off stage. He exits down the stairs from the stage as he makes his way to where both Tracy and Ryan were sitting in the audience. Joe finally reaches them as he maneuvers around the crowd of attendees. He gives Tracy a passionate hug and a kiss on the cheek, then turning to his good friend Ryan Comfort as he gives him the biggest bear hug he can muster.

Ryan, "If you kiss me like you did your wife, people are going to talk."

As Joe laughs with a loud burst, he then says, "I think I would have a lot of explaining to do to my wife. What the hell are you doing here, you son-of-a-gun."

Ryan, "I believe that it would only be appropriate that both you and I should be here to pay tribute in honoring our dear departed friend."

Joe, "You are so right. I'm so glad you were able to make it."

Ryan, "It's not just me that's here. I embody all of R&R Industries, along with all those that loved and respected Cody."

Joe, "Let me get out of this cap and gown. How long are you going to be in town, my friend?"

Ryan, "I was going to fly back home tomorrow morning."

Joe, "You got any plans for tonight? Why don't you have dinner with Tracy and I? We can tell some tall stories, so Tracy will see that it wasn't always just work, we did manage to have a little bit of fun doing what we're best at."

Ryan, "I accept."

Joe, "Good, then it's settled."

End

List of Main Characters

Joseph A. Sherman—Inventor
Main character

Tracy Sherman—Wife to Joseph A. Sherman.
Mentioned throughout parts of the novel.

Ryan Comfort—Senior Chief Engineer at R&R Industries.
Mentioned throughout parts of the novel.

Cody Banks—Electronics and Computer Engineer at R&R
Industries.
Mentioned throughout parts of the novel.

List of Side Characters

Joshua Sherman—Joe Sherman's older son mentioned in
Chapter 1.

Laura Sherman—Joe Sherman's younger daughter.
Mentioned in Chapter 1.

Morgan Sheperd—Friend and co-worker to Joe from work. mentioned in Chapter 1.

Sam Stamos—Joe's boss at work. mentioned in Chapter 1.

Nathan Silvers—Pain-in-the-butt marketing manager at work.
mentioned in Chapter 1.

Sheryl Davis—Technician in the programming lab at R&R Industries. Mentioned in Chapter 2.

Zak Taylor—Human Resources representative at R&R Industries. Mentioned in Chapter 2.

Vicky Banks—Wife of Cody Banks.
mentioned in Chapters 13, 17—no dialogue.

U.S. Army Colonel—James R. Thayer
Head of the operative group sent to R&R Industries
Addressed R&R Industries personnel in the auditorium.

R&R Technician 1—Chris Potter—R&R Industries.
In charge of onboard control console 1—T.E.O.S.
Engine systems, mentioned in Chapter 3.

R&R Technician 2—Max Seneca—R&R Industries.
In charge of onboard control console 2—T.E.O.S. engine callouts pertaining to performance parameters.
Mentioned in Chapter 3.

R&R Senior Technician—Sam Diamond—R&R Industries.
Interacts with the pilot, R&R Technicians, both Ryan Comfort and Joe Sherman. Mentioned in Chapter 3.

WFAA Channel 8, ABC Dallas TX. Rick Trauman male TV anchor. Mentioned in Chapter 4.

WFAA Channel 8, ABC Dallas TX. Joanie Sable female TV anchor. Mentioned in Chapter 4.

WFAA Channel 8, ABC field reporter – Danielle Gomez
Mentioned in Chapter 4.

WFAA Channel 8, ABC cameraman – Alex Simpkins
Mentioned in Chapter 4.

Jerome Nudel—Captain—Lufthansa *1309*
Mentioned in Chapter 4.

Hank Nisselsen—First Officer—Lufthansa *1309*
Mentioned in Chapter 4.

Trevor Martin—Anchorman 12:00 news at noon KTVD TV Station 20, Denver Co.
Mentioned in Chapter 4.

Cynthia Ashton—Anchorwoman—12:00 news at noon
KTVD TV Station 20, Denver Co.
Mentioned in Chapter 4.

Alicia Rodriquez—TV field reporter
WABC Channel 7 TV, NYC
Mentioned in Chapter 4.

Chuck Stafford—Cameraman
WABC Channel 7 TV, NYC
Mentioned in Chapter 4.

John Roberts—Captain—American Airlines *407*
Mentioned in Chapter 4

Larry Bergman—First Officer—American Airlines*407*
Mentioned in Chapter 4.

Reginald (Reggie) Chandler—N.T.S.B. lead investigator
Mentioned in Chapter 4.

Liam Eriksson—Captain—Scandinavian Airlines *145*
Mentioned in Chapter 5.

William Hurst—First Officer—Scandinavian Airlines*145*
Mentioned in Chapter 5.

Jay—passenger on Scandinavian Airlines—seat-boyfriend
to Sarah.
Jay is mentioned in Chapter 5.

Sarah—passenger on Scandinavian Airlines—seat-girlfriend to Jay.
Sarah is mentioned in Chapter 5.

Noor Kouri—Captain—Qatar Airways *334*
Mentioned in Chapter 5.

Asaad Shamoon—First Officer—Qatar Airways *334*
Mentioned in Chapter 5.

Carmen Havasta—passenger on Qatar Airway *334*—seat 14A
Husband is Ronnie. Mentioned in Chapter 5.

Ronnie Havasta—passenger on Qatar Airways *334*—seat 14B
Wife is Carmen. Ronnie is mentioned in Chapter 5.

Gregg Deland—Captain—Delta Airlines *4502*
Murdered in Chapter 6.

Jerry Lopez—First Officer—Delta Airlines *4502*
Murdered in Chapter 6.

Ellen Sillman—Senior Flight Attendant—Delta Airlines*4502*
Mentioned in Chapter 6, died on the *4502* flight

Hayyan Aboud—Terrorist #1—Delta Airlines *4502*
Suske Farhi—Terrorist #2—Delta Airlines *4502*
Joram Hakim—Terrorist #3—Delta Airlines *4502*

Salem Abdul—Terrorist #4—Delta Airlines *4502*
The above four terrorist were killed on the *4502* flight.

Jason Santini—United States Army Sergeant on leave
Wounded by Suske, Chapter 6, killed on the *4502* flight.

Renee LeBeau—Captain—Air France 706
Drugged in Chapter 7 and presumed killed on the *706* flight.

Roberta Bernard—First Officer—Air France *706*.
Drugged in Chapter 7 and presumed killed on the *706* flight.

Milad Isa—Terrorist Pilot—Air France *706*
Killed in Chapter 7.

Ali Sarraf—Terrorist First Officer—Air France 706
Killed in Chapter 7.

Kasim Daher—Third Terrorist—Air France *706*
Killed in Chapter 7.

Flight Attendant Muhammad Tohan—Air France *706*
survived in Chapter 7.

Peter Kowalski—Air Traffic Controller—Warsaw
Chopin Airport. Mentioned in Chapter 7.

Alex Nowak—Lead Air Traffic Controller—Warsaw
Chopin Airport. Mentioned in Chapter 7.

Jan Lewinski—Captain—Commanding Officer, 33rd Air Base
Powidz, Poland
Mentioned in chapter 7.

Retired British Army Staff Sergeant Reginald
(Reggie) Upton
Survived in Chapter 7.

Mrs. Emma Caron—Lead B.E.A. Investigator—
AirFrance*706*
Mentioned in Chapter 7.

Jacques Fournier—E.A.S.A. Senior Member—Air
France 706
Mentioned in Chapter 7.

Jackson Elliot—lead investigator N.T.S.B.
Washington D.C.
Mentioned in Chapter 8.

Rachael Hart—Assistant to Marshall Collins—F.A.A.
Mentioned in Chapter 8.

Xavier Fitzgerald—Administrator for T.S.A.
(Transportation Security Administration)
Mentioned in Chapter 8.

Tim Hodges—Junior Assistant—Homeland Security—
under T.S.A. official Xavier Fitzgerald
Mentioned in Chapter 8.

Ajit Ramon—Cab driver in Washington D.C.
Mentioned in Chapter 9.

James Easterson—Captain—British Airway *235*
Mentioned in Chapter 11.

Loretta Parker—First Officer—British Airway *235*
Mentioned in Chapter 11.

Nancy Houston—Senior Flight Attendant
British Airway *235*
Mentioned in Chapter 11.

Omar Sultan—Lead Terrorist—British Airways *235*
Mentioned in Chapter 11.

Khalil Aman—Second terrorist—British Airways*235*
Mentioned in Chapter 11.

Shah Nasir—Third terrorist—British Airways *235*
Mentioned in Chapter 11.

Lt. Major Maxwell (Max) Logan—U.S. Air Force Pilot
Mentioned in Chapter 12.

Captain Perry Addams—U.S. Air Force Co-Pilot
Mentioned in Chapter 12.

Dr. Nelson Franklin—Director of McMurdo Station
Mentioned in Chapter 12.

Gerry Hathaway—Research Assistant—McMurdo Station
Mentioned in Chapter 12.

Dr. Elli McPhenson—Climatologist—McMurdo research
facility, Antarctica.
Mentioned in Chapter 12.

Jim Gears—Researcher—McMurdo Station
Mentioned in Chapter 12.

Dr. John Evans—Base Doctor—McMurdo Station
Mentioned in Chapter 12.

Stewart Kilpatrick—Captain—Spirit Airlines *1666*
Mentioned in Chapter 13.

Danny Smith—First Officer—Spirit Airlines *1666*
Mentioned in Chapter 13.

Shelley—Receptionist—N.T.S.B.
Mentioned in Chapter 14.

Henry Boyd—Lead investigator, N.T.S.B.
Mentioned in Chapter 14.

Samuel Cohen—Senior Director, F.A.A.
Mentioned in Chapter 14.

Jake Lewis—Captain—Savin Air Vermont Express
Mentioned in Chapter 15 and 16.

Marty Simmons—First Officer—Savin Air Vermont Express
Mentioned in Chapter 15 and 16.

Cy Newman—Cargo Master—Savin Air Vermont Express
Mentioned in Chapter 15 and 16.

John Gormley—Cargo Master—Savin Air Vermont Express
Mentioned in Chapter 15 and 16.

Paul Savin—CEO and President—Savin Air Vermont Express
Mentioned in Chapter 15 and 16.

Sid Bloomberg—Flight OPS Manager—Savin Air Vermont Express
Mentioned in Chapter 15.

Andy—F.A.A. Mechanic Northeast Kingdom International airport
Mentioned in Chapter 15.

Noah—C.A.S.A. Engine Mechanic—Brisbane Airport
Mentioned in Chapter 15.

Jack Wilson—Director—Brisbane Airport
Mentioned in Chapter 16.

Samantha Gibbons—Channel 7 Reporter—Brisbane
Mentioned in Chapter 16.

84 side characters mentioned plus two not named.

On the Bad guy side is: That maybe a matter of opinion as far as a bad guy is concerned.
Mr. R.—United States government covert operative

Abbreviations used in the book

T.E.O.S.: Thrust Enabling Objective System
USPTO: United States Patent and Trademark Office
A.I.U.: Air Injection Unit (part of T.E.O.S.)
N.T.S.B.: National Transportation Safety Board
F.A.A.: Federal Aviation Administration

IFR: Instrument Flight Rules—means by which allocations taken by the flight crew in control is accomplished with the use of gauges and instruments instead of relying on visual sightings to acquire location of where the aircraft is at in a given airspace.

IGS: Icelandic Geological Society
TSA: Transportation Security Administration
BEA: Bureau of Enquiry and Analysis
EASA: European Aviation Safety Agency
GPS: Global Positioning System
GPU: Ground Power Unit
APU: Auxiliary Power Unit
UPS: United Parcel Service

Definitions used in the book

Port — Known as the left side of an aircraft or water vessel. Starboard: Known as the right side of an aircraft or water vessel. Yaw: a twisting or oscillation of a moving ship or aircraft around a vertical axis.

ATC — Air Traffic Control.

Spatial-Temporal — is used in data analysis when data is collected across both space and time.

3D Printer: Is the construction of a three-dimensional object from a CAD model or a digital 3D model.

Autobots — Are benevolent, sentient, self-configuring robotic lifeforms from the planet Cybertron.

F22 Raptor — Lockheed Martin F-22 Raptor is an American single-seat, twin-engine, all-weather stealth tactical fighter aircraft.

Algorithm — a process or set of rules to be followed in calculations especially by a computer.

C++ Programming — A general-purpose programming computer language.

LED — Light emitting diode (a electronic component that can conduct electric current in only one direction.) Humerus: Is a long bone in the arm that runs from the shoulder to the elbow.

Wingbox — Primary load carrying structure of a fixed wing aircraft. Used to connect each wing to the fuselage.

Tibia — The main bone of the lower leg, forming what is more commonly known as the shin.

9 781643 787978